THE CLUE OF
The Black Keys

Books by

CAROLYN KEENE

Nancy Drew Mystery Stories

Dana Girls Mystery Stories

Was the handkerchief a signal of distress?

The Clue of the Black Keys

NANCY DREW MYSTERY STORIES

THE CLUE OF
The Black Keys

BY CAROLYN KEENE

NEW YORK

Grosset & Dunlap

PUBLISHERS

Contents

THE CLUE OF
The Black Keys

CHAPTER I

An Urgent Request

Nancy Drew's eyes sparkled as she and Bess Marvin stepped from the afternoon plane.

"It was a grand week end in New York," Nancy said. "But it's good to be back in River Heights. There's your mother, Bess."

Mrs. Marvin kissed the girls and offered Nancy a ride home.

"Thank you," she answered, "but I left my car here."

As the slender, blond girl walked toward the parking lot, a young man in a gray topcoat signaled her to wait. His worried look and the urgency of his pace gave Nancy the feeling something was wrong.

"You are Nancy Drew?" he asked. When she nodded, he said, "Your father—"

"Is Dad—is something the matter?" Nancy interrupted fearfully.

"I'm sorry. I didn't mean to frighten you.

1

Your father is all right. But I'm concerned about a friend of mine," the stranger went on. "I consulted your father about him this morning. Mr. Drew said my case sounded more like a mystery for a detective than for a lawyer!"

Nancy studied the eager young man. He was not more than twenty-five, she decided, tall and attractive looking, with serious, blue eyes and reddish hair.

"Perhaps I should introduce myself," he said. "My name is Scott—Terence Scott, but my friends call me Terry. I'm on the faculty of Keystone University. You may think it's strange, my coming to meet you here. But when I learned how clever you are at solving mysteries—"

"I'll do what I can," Nancy promised.

Terry Scott picked up her suitcase. "Couldn't we discuss things more comfortably if I ride home with you?" he asked.

Nancy hesitated. The young man appeared to be honest, but she had learned to be wary of all strangers until she had proof of their identity.

"It's quite comfortable in the waiting room," she said. "Suppose we go in there and you tell me your story."

She preceded him into the building and found a secluded bench beyond a group of waiting passengers.

Terry Scott removed his topcoat, folded it, and placed it on the bench between them.

"The story," he said, "begins in Mexico," and though his voice was low, Nancy caught the pulse of excitement in his words.

"A group of professors," he went on, "were working together last summer to unravel an ancient mystery. I was in that group. Our search led us to an unexplored section of Mexico, where we planned to dig for a treasure."

"Yes?" Nancy said, her interest now thoroughly aroused.

"According to old legends, something of great benefit to mankind is secreted with the treasure. We professors, Dr. Graham, Dr. Pitt, Dr. Anderson and myself, are as interested in finding out what this is as we are in finding the treasure."

"You have no idea what it is?" Nancy asked excitedly.

Terry Scott shook his head. "But after weeks of excavating, Dr. Pitt and I did come across a clue which the four of us were sure would lead to the treasure."

Terry Scott leaned forward, his face tense with eagerness.

"It was a stone tablet. We knew at once that all we needed to do was translate the cipher on it, and the secret would be ours. But then something terrible happened."

"What?"

"The night after our find, Dr. Pitt and the stone tablet disappeared!"

"He stole it?" Nancy asked, shocked.

Terry Scott frowned. "I don't know. **Dr. Pitt** was pretty secretive. He was a bachelor, and closemouthed about his work. But a fine man, and all the professors would swear he's honest."

"Perhaps he was the victim of foul play," Nancy suggested. "Did you call in the police?"

"Yes. They haven't turned up a thing, but I feel that Dr. Pitt is alive."

"Being held captive somewhere?" Nancy offered.

Terry Scott shrugged. "Whatever it is, I mean to get to the bottom of it. Dr. Pitt must be found. And I don't intend that any impostor shall get the credit for something that belongs to us professors!" The young man's eyes blazed.

"I can't blame you," Nancy agreed. "Have you any clues to help solve this mystery?"

"Yes. After Dr. Pitt disappeared, I found a couple of things in his tent that I believe are important. Here is one of them."

He reached deep into a pocket of his topcoat and brought out an object wrapped in tissue paper. It was the bottom half of a large antique key, black in color and of an unusual luster.

"There were three of these keys originally," he explained, "all made of obsidian."

"That's glass, isn't it?" Nancy asked.

"Yes, a kind of volcanic glass," Terry Scott

answered. "The other keys disappeared when Dr. Pitt did."

He held the curious half-key up to the light for Nancy's examination, then returned it to the pocket of his topcoat.

"We'll need that half-key before we're through," he stated. "But, in the meantime, I figure what we ought to do is find a man named Juarez Tino."

"Why?" Nancy asked.

Terry Scott said that he suspected this man and his wife of being thieves. They had been working near the Mexican camp site for some time before the stone tablet had been found.

"The Tinos passed themselves off as scientists, but my guess is they're fakers. The same day Dr. Pitt, the cipher stone, and the keys disappeared, they vanished."

"You think Dr. Pitt went off with them?" Nancy remarked.

"Either with them or after them. I believe if we can trace Juarez Tino and his wife, we'll find Dr. Joshua Pitt as well as solve our ancient mystery."

"Oh, I hope so," said Nancy. "Did any of you make a copy of the cipher on the stone tablet?"

The young man shook his head ruefully. "I wish we had. If only one of us had made a rubbing of the stone and hidden it somewhere. But we found the tablet at the end of the day when we were tired. We never thought it might be stolen before morning!"

Suddenly Terry Scott glanced at his wrist watch. "I almost forgot," he exclaimed. "I promised Dr. Graham I'd telephone him. The old man gets very upset if he's kept waiting. Excuse me for a moment, please."

Leaving his coat at Nancy's side, Terry Scott dashed off to a telephone booth around the corner. Nancy waited, pondering the strange events he had related.

She did not notice a dark, swarthy man eying her from among a group of travelers. When he sauntered over and took Scott's place on the bench, she did not even glance his way.

Suddenly, out of the corner of her eye, Nancy saw the swarthy man fingering Scott's topcoat.

"What are you doing?" she cried, and snatched the coat from his grasp.

The man stood up hastily and hurried toward a side door. Just as he disappeared outside, Terry Scott returned. He noticed Nancy's look of apprehension.

"Is something wrong?" he asked anxiously.

"I'm not sure," Nancy answered. "A man who came to sit here acted as if he wanted to steal your coat."

A look of alarm came over the young professor's face. "What did the man look like?" he asked.

"Dark, short," she replied. "Sort of a crooked mouth and beady eyes."

"That sounds like Juarez Tino, the man I was telling you about!" Frantically, Terry Scott snatched up his coat and plunged a hand into the inner pocket. "It's gone!" he gasped. "Juarez has the black key!"

"We'll go after him!" Nancy jumped up and rushed for the door through which the man had gone.

Terry dashed after her, and they hailed a blue-coated policeman. Nancy recognized him as Sergeant Malloy of the River Heights police force.

"Sergeant," she asked excitedly, "did you see a short, dark man come out of the waiting room?"

"You mean the one that was running, Miss Drew? He just drove off in that blue sedan with another fellow." Malloy waved toward a departing car.

"He's a thief! We must stop him!" Nancy cried.

Asking the policeman to follow her and Terry Scott, she raced for her car. The two men piled in beside her, and they sped off.

Nancy drove northward along the main highway toward River Heights, and at last came close enough to note that the sedan ahead had a Florida license plate. Then, at a busy intersection, she was stopped by a traffic light and lost sight of the other car.

"Keep pushing," Malloy directed her, when the light changed. "They're up ahead some place. We'll find 'em in town."

A few minutes later Terry Scott pointed excitedly. "They just passed us—going the other way!" he cried. "They're heading back to the airport!"

Nancy maneuvered her car in a neat U turn and took up the chase again. The sedan was well ahead, but Nancy kept gaining. Surely, steadily, her car drew closer. Another quarter mile and they would overtake Juarez Tino.

But just as they approached the far side of the airfield, the blue sedan suddenly swerved from the road. Swaying dizzily, it swung across a rough field and onto the runway. Nancy started to follow, then jammed on her brakes. The car screeched to a stop, but the sedan kept on directly in the path of an incoming transport plane.

"There'll be a crash!" Nancy cried out in horror.

CHAPTER II

A Suspect Escapes

NANCY covered her face with her hands, expecting to hear the ripping, grinding sound of a collision. Instead, she heard Terry Scott shout:

"They made it!"

Looking up, Nancy saw the plane taxiing along the runway.

"That crazy driver just missed by the skin of his teeth!" Malloy exclaimed.

"Somebody's getting out of the car," Nancy remarked.

"I'll get him," the sergeant said, opening the door.

"I'll go with you," Nancy offered.

"Better not, Miss Drew," came the answer. "It's too dangerous on the runway."

Nancy bit her lip in vexation, but obeyed him. From her first mystery, *The Secret of the Old Clock*, through her most recent, *The Secret of the Wooden Lady*, Nancy, still in her teens, had mixed courage

and daring beyond her years. Still, her father
and others of his generation out of devotion frequently had held her back. So now she obeyed
Sergeant Malloy and waited in the car.

As the officer reached the sedan on the runway,
a man stepped out of it.

"Must be the driver," Terry Scott commented.
"He's too tall for Juarez."

The policeman leaned inside. Apparently
Juarez was not in sight.

"He's not there. Juarez got out of the car and
escaped!" Nancy gasped.

"With that key of mine, the scoundrel!" Terry
fumed. "I'd like to get my hands on him!"

Nancy tossed back a blond lock and frowned.
Then she turned to her companion. "Are you
sure Juarez was in the sedan when it passed us
on the road?"

"Certainly. Both men were on the front seat."

"Then Juarez must be here at the airport,"
Nancy declared.

With one hand shielding her eyes from the
glare of the sun, she studied the tall grass that
fringed the far side of the runway.

"Look!" she cried suddenly. "He's running
through the grass toward the airport building!"

Nancy turned her key in the ignition lock,
backed onto the road, and headed for the building. Traffic was heavy, and she chafed at the
delay, but finally she made it.

As Nancy parked, she and Terry heard the roar of an outgoing plane. A crowd of onlookers were waving good-by.

"Must be that Florida Special I saw chalked up on the flight board," Terry remarked.

Florida! An idea flashed into Nancy's mind. The plane was bound for Florida—and the license on the blue sedan was Florida! Was there a connection?

"Let's go to the ticket office and inquire about the passengers," she said excitedly. "Juarez Tino might be on that plane!"

Nancy quickly gained the attention of a clerk.

"May I see the list of passengers who boarded the Florida plane?" she asked the girl.

"Certainly."

She was handed a typewritten sheet. Six passengers had boarded the plane at River Heights. Juarez Tino was not one of them.

"Did all the passengers with reservations claim their seats?" Nancy asked.

The girl at the counter chuckled. "Yes, all the passengers got on. But one of them almost didn't make it. He came rushing up at the last minute, out of breath."

Nancy leaned forward excitedly. "What was his name? Please tell me. I have a particular reason for knowing."

The clerk tried hard to remember. Then she pointed to a name on the list. "Conway King.

His wife kept fidgeting around, worrying where her husband was and saying things about him in a loud, brassy voice."

"Did you see her husband when he came in?"

The clerk shook her head. "He went right out to the plane. Somebody said he made it all right. That's all I know."

"Thank you," Nancy said, and turned away. When she and Terry Scott were alone, she said quietly, "Do you think Juarez might be using the name Conway King?"

"It's quite possible. And that 'brassy voice' certainly sounds like his wife. I think we should inform the police so Juarez can be questioned at the next stop."

Nancy looked at the flight schedule which had not yet been erased. "The plane won't come down for two hours. Before we tell the police, I think we should make a thorough search for the key."

Her companion looked puzzled. "Search? What do you mean?"

Nancy smiled. "When I first started helping my father on his cases, he gave me some good advice. He said, 'If you want to be a good detective, consider all the possibilities. Don't jump to conclusions.' "

"Well, I don't see that we're jumping to any conclusions," Terry Scott said in surprise. "Juarez stole that key of mine, and if he's on the plane, the police ought to nab him and get it back."

"When you didn't find the key in your pocket, we both thought Juarez had stolen it," Nancy reminded him. "But maybe—"

She did not finish the sentence. Beckoning him to follow her, Nancy walked over to the bench which they had occupied earlier. Wasn't it possible Juarez had dropped the key in his haste to leave? He might even have hidden it, intending to come back later.

Hurriedly, Nancy looked along the top of the bench. No key there. And it was not on the floor underneath. Finally she turned to Terry Scott, who was also searching.

"Are you sure you didn't take that key into the phone booth with you?"

"I'm quite certain. But I'll look just the same."

While he was gone, Nancy examined the floor from the bench to the side door through which Juarez had made his exit. She looked on the ground outside the door. No key.

Disappointed, she returned to the bench and sat down. Suddenly Nancy realized that the dark wooden seat was not solid, but built of strips about half an inch apart.

With renewed hope she felt along the cracks of the smooth wood. Her little finger felt something. Looking closely, Nancy saw an irregular black object wedged between the boards!

Terry Scott's antique half-key!

Taking a nail file from her purse, Nancy dug out the relic and presented it to the young man upon his return. He could hardly believe his good fortune.

"You were right," he admitted. "I did jump to conclusions. And you're a good detective. I'm sure that from now on our case will prosper."

"I'm afraid I haven't been very helpful so far," Nancy replied. "I was only two feet from the man you want to catch, and let him get away!"

"But you proved something," Terry Scott insisted. "I know now that Juarez is on my trail. He probably has learned about the half-key and means to steal it. Also, you discovered that he's on his way to Florida with his wife, and that they travel under an assumed name."

"We don't know that," Nancy reminded him. "We're only guessing."

The young professor laughed. "Now I know you're a lawyer's daughter. That careful, logical mind! Well, how about it? Will you stay on the case and help me solve my puzzle?"

Nancy's curiosity was thoroughly aroused. Unlocking a secret of antiquity presented a new kind of mystery! That strange half-key. The disappearance of Dr. Pitt and the stolen cipher. Scheming Juarez Tino and his unpleasant wife. They were all intriguing to a girl like Nancy.

She was tempted to say, "Yes, of course I'll

help you." But nice as Terry Scott seemed, she must check on him first. Nancy decided to talk the matter over with her father.

"If you'll tell me where you're staying, I promise to let you know," she replied. "I'll telephone tomorrow morning."

Reluctantly the young man accepted her decision, saying he was staying at the Claymore. Then, after thanking her, he went to call a taxicab.

Nancy felt a pang of regret. The afternoon's chase had been exciting. Deep in her heart she longed to solve the mystery. Not only was the prospect intriguing, but it would be fun to work with Terry Scott, she was sure.

"But right now I'd better get home," she thought, "and see Dad."

As Nancy crossed the parking lot toward her car, she heard a shout. Sergeant Malloy was sternly leading an angry, gesticulating man. Nancy recognized him as Juarez's companion—the man who had driven the blue sedan.

"Arrest me, will you?" he roared. "It's this girl—you said her name's Nancy Drew—she's the one you ought to arrest!"

CHAPTER III

A Midnight Scare

NANCY looked at the heavy-set man in amazement. Sergeant Malloy protested, "Come, now. What do you have against Miss Drew?"

"Plenty," he answered, his gray-green eyes flashing. "She's the one that chased me like I was a criminal. She sent you to embarrass me. Look how everybody's staring at me, as if I was going to jail. She's hurt my good name."

"What is your name?" Nancy asked coolly.

"It's a good name!" shouted the man defiantly. "I've been doing business in River Heights and people know me. They think I'm fine. Now what will they say? My reputation is worth money. My business—"

"What kind of business?" interrupted the sergeant.

"I sell citrus fruit for the Tropical Sun Fruit Company of Florida. Is there anything wrong with that? Have I broken the law, being a fruit salesman?"

By this time the man's loud voice and angry gestures had drawn even more of a crowd. People waited to see what was going to happen.

Nancy flushed. Still, she thought, there was something so exaggerated about the man's rage that it did not make sense.

"*He's hiding something—something he doesn't want us to know.*"

Sergeant Malloy grumbled, "Let's see your driver's license and car registration."

The man thrust them under Malloy's nose. Nancy and the sergeant studied them together. The license and registration were made out to Wilfred Porterly, Miami, Florida.

"All right, Mr. Porterly," said the sergeant. "I'm not pinning anything on you—yet. Just tell me one thing. Where's your friend?"

"Juarez Tino," Nancy added.

Porterly blinked and hesitated, then said, "Juarez? I don't know any Juarez. Any Tino either."

"How about the man who rode in your car? Is his name Conway King?" Nancy asked.

The man's eyes narrowed. "Maybe it is; maybe it ain't. How should I know? He was a stranger. I never saw him before. He begged a ride."

The man's voice became quieter now, almost wheedling. "I didn't know the fellow, officer. He was here at the airport; told me he'd left some important papers at his hotel. Couldn't find a taxi, so he begged me to take him back to town.

"After he picked up his papers, I drove him back here to the airport. He made me drive onto the field so he wouldn't miss his plane. It was a short cut."

"And you nearly killed yourself and thirty plane passengers just to accommodate a stranger?" Malloy said sarcastically.

"It wasn't my fault. He grabbed the wheel."

Nancy pretended surprise. "You say Juarez took the wheel?"

"Sure. I mean—I don't know what his name was. He said he had to catch the plane."

Porterly must have felt that his words had trapped him. He turned his fury on Nancy.

"You're responsible. If there'd been a crash, you'd have been to blame. I suppose you think you're a detective!" he scoffed.

"Nancy Drew," stated a firm, angry voice from the crowd, "is a very good detective. You'd better be careful what you say about her."

Nancy turned in astonishment. An athletic-looking, dark-haired girl was striding toward her. She was Nancy's friend, George Fayne. With her was pretty, dimpled Bess Marvin, her cousin.

"What is it all about?" Bess whispered, when they reached Nancy's side. "I found I'd left my hatbox, so I asked George to drive back here with me."

"Tell you later," said Nancy in a low voice.

"You'd better quiet down," the sergeant was telling Porterly, "or I'll arrest you for disturbing the peace. Sell all the grapefruit you want, but behave yourself. I'll be watching you."

Porterly hesitated. Then, with a baleful look, he turned and walked rapidly toward his sedan.

Sergeant Malloy spoke to the crowd. "All right, folks, break it up." With a wave of his hand at Nancy and her friends, he strode toward the airport office.

George Fayne watched the disappearing figure of the blustering Porterly.

"Hypers, Nancy," she scolded, "you do get mixed up with the wickedest-looking characters. Who in the world was that one?"

Nancy laughed. "We were playing Cops and Robbers," she answered, "and Mr. Porterly didn't care for the game." Nancy took the two girls by the hand. "Oh, I *am* glad I have friends like you two," she said. "You have such a nice way of popping up from nowhere when I'm in trouble."

Bess was not smiling. "Nancy, you aren't mixed up in another mystery before you even get home!" she exclaimed.

"Well," Nancy confessed slowly, "I'm not sure."

George Fayne groaned. "We know how it'll be. The youngest and loveliest detective in River Heights will shortly turn a deaf ear on invitations to art classes, football games, dances—"

"You sillies," Nancy said, smiling. "I never turn down an invitation to dance and you know it!"

The three girls walked together to Nancy's car, and she stepped in. As her two friends leaned against the door, talking, George dramatically put up a hand for silence.

"We have company," she whispered. "A man."

"Not that awful Mr. Porterly?" Bess squealed.

"Hardly," George said. "If I'm not near-sighted, he's television's dream hero in a gray topcoat."

"*Terry Scott*," thought Nancy.

She looked through the rear window of her car. It was Terry, hurrying toward her and waving an arm.

"You can't get rid of a bad penny," the young man declared when he reached Nancy.

Graciously, she introduced him to Bess and George, saying he was a professor at Keystone University.

Bess daintily disciplined her hair with her finger tips. "I'd *love* to have him for *my* professor," she thought, and noticed a twinkle in

George's eyes, which seemed to say the same thing.

"I'm sorry about that rumpus with Porterly," Terry went on. "I was in the station trying to call a taxi. I heard the shouts, but I hadn't any idea you were involved. I came right out when the sergeant told me."

"No harm done," said Nancy. "My friends here came to my defense."

"And we mean to keep on defending you until we get you safely home," George promised.

Terry grinned. "Since your friends mean to protect you so well, perhaps you'll drive me to my hotel. Every public taxi in this town seems to be busy."

"I guess it'll be safe," Nancy replied, laughing. "Climb in."

As the car rolled toward River Heights, Bess and George kept directly in back of her. When she pulled up in front of the Claymore, Terry reached into his pocket and brought out the tissue-wrapped half-key.

"I want you to keep this for me," he said, "both as a pledge of my integrity and because I no longer dare keep it myself."

"You mean someone like Juarez might steal it?" Nancy asked.

Terry nodded and said, "This key must never get in the hands of the wrong people."

The young professor paused. When he spoke again, Nancy was surprised at the emotion in his voice.

"In giving you this key, I'm placing in your trust the most priceless object in my possession."

He was silent for a moment. Nancy said nothing, waiting for him to continue.

"Please take my case," he went on. "I believe that you are the person who can solve it. As soon as you agree, I'll give you all the details. But we will have to work quickly."

"I understand," Nancy replied. She hesitated to take the key until she knew him better, but she decided to show it to her father when she asked his advice about the case. Aloud she said, "You'll hear from me tomorrow."

Nancy slipped the relic into her shoulder bag. As Terry entered his hotel, Bess and George pulled up alongside her.

"Lucky you!" Bess called out, winking at Nancy.

"He's charming," George teased. "Tonight I'm sending an application to Keystone University!"

"Stop it, girls," Nancy pleaded, then added with a grin, "But he is handsome, isn't he?"

Without waiting for a reply, she started her car, waving good-by to Bess and George as she threaded her way through the traffic. She was still wondering about the obsidian key, and what mystery it might unlock, when she arrived home ten minutes later.

Her father, Carson Drew, and the housekeeper, Hannah Gruen, who had taken care of the home since Mrs. Drew's death many years before, greeted her at the door. After kissing them both, she led the way into the living room.

"From the clutch you have on that purse of yours, Nancy," Mr. Drew said laughingly, "you must have brought a treasure from New York."

"It may lead to one," Nancy declared.

She showed him the strange object, asking if he had ever seen anything like it before.

"No."

"Dad, do you know a Terence Scott?"

"I just met him this morning. He was at my office. What made you ask?"

"This key is his. He met me at the plane."

Mr. Drew's eyes widened. "Well, come to think of it, I did say you were arriving by plane, but I had no idea—"

"How much do you know about him?" Nancy questioned her father.

"Practically nothing."

"Dad, will you please call up Keystone University and ask what he teaches and what they think of him?"

"Gladly, Detective Drew." Her father smiled.

Nancy gave him a hug. "Oh, Dad, there's so much to tell—"

"But not now," said Hannah Gruen. She was trying to look stern, but devotion shone in every line of her honest, motherly face as she added, "I've been saving supper for you, and if you don't sit down real soon, it'll be burned to a cinder."

"Supper!" cried Nancy. "That's a lovely idea. I'll be ready in two jiffs."

She hurried upstairs. Before she even smoothed her wind-blown curls, Nancy took the black key from her purse and hid it among sachets and handkerchiefs in a small drawer of her dressing table.

"It should be safe there for the present," she decided.

During supper Nancy told about her week end and the exciting events that had taken place at the airport.

Mr. Drew said that he knew the elderly Dr. Pitt with whom the mysterious Terry Scott claimed to have been in Mexico. He had not had time to check the young man's story.

"Then, Dad," Nancy said as they arose, "will you please check on him right away?"

The call was put through to Keystone University. After a slight delay, Mr. Drew was connected with the president's home, and frankly presented his questions. In a few minutes the conversation was over.

"The report is, Nancy, that Terence Scott is an outstanding young professor, who has a leave of absence this year and went to Mexico last summer on an exploring expedition."

"Then his story is true!" Nancy exclaimed. "Dad, is there any reason why I shouldn't help him on the case?"

"I can't give my answer to that question until I make a further investigation." Mr. Drew could not be dissuaded from this decision.

Nancy retired, still trying to account for the strange happenings of the day. But her head was hardly upon the pillow, before she fell fast asleep.

It was past midnight when she heard, even in her dreams, a stealthy, crunching sound. Her mind struggled to awaken.

"Something is happening," she realized. "It's not a dream, it's going on now."

Something, somebody was moving stealthily about Nancy's room. A dim, dark-clad figure was creeping toward her bed!

CHAPTER IV

Clue in a Triangle

FOR A MOMENT Nancy did not move nor make a sound. Then, with courage, she reached toward her bedside table and switched on the light.

There stood Hannah Gruen. The woman's face was drawn and white.

"What's the matter?" Nancy whispered.

The housekeeper put a finger to her lips, as she glanced suspiciously around the room. Then she looked out the window. Finally she signaled Nancy to put on a robe and follow her into the hall.

"I heard footsteps on the stairs," Mrs. Gruen whispered. "I wanted to make sure you were all right."

They heard Mr. Drew come out to the hall. In his hand he held a golf club ready to use as a weapon.

"Hannah," he ordered, "stay close to Nancy,

You two look around the rooms up here. I'm
going downstairs. Yell if you find anyone."

She and Nancy looked through each room,
searching closets, peering under beds, and examining the lawyer's study carefully. Everything
seemed to be normal.

"Dad's calling us," said Nancy a few minutes
later.

Hurrying downstairs, they found Mr. Drew in
the living room. He was looking at the window
next to the piano.

"It's been jimmied," he said.

"Do you suppose somebody's still in the house?"
Mrs. Gruen asked.

"I think that whoever it was got away," Carson
Drew concluded, pointing outside the window.
In the soft earth close to a rosebush, they saw a
man's footprints.

"Our silverware!" the housekeeper gasped.

"Don't worry. I checked that," Mr. Drew
said. "Nothing was disturbed."

"The black key!" thought Nancy.

Racing back upstairs, she made sure it was still
there and breathed a sigh of relief.

"I'm glad I didn't leave it downstairs," she
told herself.

Every place that had not been searched before
was investigated, in case the intruder had an ac-
complice still hiding in the house. But there was
no intruder on the premises.

"It's too bad your dog Togo wasn't here, Nancy," Hannah said. "He would have taken care of the burglar!"

At the moment Togo, Nancy's terrier, was with Mr. Drew's sister. She had asked if she might take him to keep her company while spending a three-weeks' vacation at her summer home.

After such an exciting night, it was not surprising that Nancy slept late next morning. When she came downstairs at nine o'clock, she found Bess Marvin waiting for her. Bess drew up a chair and chatted excitedly while Nancy ate breakfast.

"Mrs. Gruen told me all about last night," Bess began, "and I think she's absolutely right. If you take Terry Scott's case, something awful is bound to happen to you."

Nancy raised her eyebrows. "Why, Bess, I thought you liked him," and she laughed when her friend blushed.

"Oh, I do," Bess protested. "He's nice, and he's awfully handsome. I wish you could help him, but—"

"But what?"

"Well, it seems so dangerous. And Ned Nickerson won't like it a bit. He'll be so worried, Nancy, especially when he takes a look at your professor!"

"Bess!" exclaimed Nancy, smiling. "Ned won't think anything of the sort!"

As she finished a glass of milk, the telephone rang. "Nancy, it's for you," Hannah announced.

The person on the telephone was Terry Scott. His voice sounded hoarse and excited. "Is everything all right?" he asked.

"Oh, yes. Quite safe," she assured him, thinking he meant the key.

Terry seemed to be speaking with an effort. "Will you be there all morning, in case I want to see you?"

"I'll be here," Nancy promised. "Has something happened?"

"Yes. Something serious. When I came up to my hotel room last night, a visitor was waiting for me in the clothes closet. He struck me on the head and I didn't come to until six o'clock this morning."

"How dreadful!" Nancy gasped. "What did he look like?"

"I don't know. All I saw was a mask."

"Did he steal anything?"

"He certainly did. Rifled my pockets and took most of my notes on that Mexican expedition. I planned to use them for a lecture I'm giving soon."

"Did he take anything else?"

"Apparently not. He did a fine job, though, on my suitcase. Dumped everything I own on the floor."

Terry decided he had better say no more on the telephone. "I'll come over later and talk to you," he suggested.

"All right. I'll be here."

When Nancy told Bess what had happened, the girl's eyes grew wide with excitement. "Do you suppose he's the same thief who came to your house last night?" she exclaimed.

"I've thought of that," said Nancy, and told where the black half-key was hidden.

A chill ran down Bess's spine. What if the same assailant had entered Nancy's room and given her the same treatment Terry had received!

"I ought to tell Dad," Nancy said, starting for the telephone. As she started to dial, Carson Drew himself walked down the stairs.

"Good morning, girls," he said.

"Dad!" Nancy exclaimed as the lawyer bent down to kiss her cheek. "I thought you'd gone to the office."

"Not this morning," Mr. Drew replied, smiling. "I have news for you, but I wanted Hannah to give you a good breakfast first."

"You two conspirators!" cried Nancy, but she took his arm affectionately and led him to his favorite chair in the living room.

"I have news, too," she said, and she related what Terry Scott had told her over the telephone.

"Too bad," the lawyer remarked.

"Now tell us your news," Nancy urged him.

"It's about the same young man," the lawyer explained. "What you have just told me complicates matters still more. You recall that I hinted to you on the phone just before you left New York about doing a little detective work for me?"

"Yes, Dad."

Before he could continue, they heard a car enter the driveway. A taxicab pulled up.

"My news will have to wait," he said.

Nancy hurried into the hall. "It's Terry Scott," she called, as she opened the door.

The pale young man, a bandage on his head, entered the living room and smiled wryly. "Good morning," he said. "I'm afraid I don't look very presentable."

"Oh, it was dreadful, that man assaulting you," Bess spoke up, concern in her voice.

"Sorry to hear it," added Mr. Drew. "Any clue to your attacker?"

"No," Terry replied. "Neither the hotel manager nor the police can account for it."

"And what do *you* think?" Nancy asked him.

The young scientist shrugged. "If Juarez Tino hadn't gone to Florida, I'd suspect him. But I can't think of anyone else."

Softhearted Bess decided to change the subject to something more pleasant. "Terry, do you speak any of the Mexican languages?" she asked.

"Why, yes, I do. Spanish, and a couple of Indian dialects. I guess that's one of the reasons

Dr. Pitt and the others chose me to go along to Mexico."

"Nancy says you almost found a fortune down there," Bess purred. "What was it?"

Terry smiled. "I suspect the treasure will be one or more frogs."

"Frogs?" cried the two girls together.

The young professor nodded. "In certain ancient civilizations the frog was sacred, just as the cow is sacred in many parts of India today. Because of its religious meaning, the frog symbol was used frequently by artists and craftsmen.

"Many of these frogs were made of silver, some of them inlaid with precious stones. A collection of such jeweled pieces would be worth a fortune."

"How did you learn about the—the frogs?" Bess asked.

"An ancient monument in Mexico carries a message in an unknown language," Terry answered. "It's all in pictures. The Indians call it the Mystery Stone, and say it tells where a fabulous treasure is buried. The Frog Treasure, it's called, and according to legend it's locked away in silver by three 'magic' obsidian keys."

"And I have half of one?" Nancy asked excitedly.

Terry nodded. "I'm hoping against hope that the treasure can't be unlocked without the missing piece, even if the treasure is found."

"Please tell the whole story from the beginning," Bess begged. "Couldn't any Mexicans read the Mystery Stone?"

"No. They only knew the legend. Late one afternoon Dr. Pitt and I dug up a small stone tablet—the one I told you about, Nancy. From photographs we had of the Mystery Stone monument, we saw that one side of the tablet had the same picture writing as the monument.

"On the reverse side of the tablet the ciphers had been translated into one of the ancient Indian dialects, which I knew. Now, with the help of the tablet we could solve the mystery! But, as you know, the tablet vanished before we had a chance to work on it."

"What about the three keys? Where did you find them?" Nancy asked.

"They were on a silver ring which was fastened to the tablet through a hole bored in one end of it. I knew at once that they were the 'magic' keys of the legend."

"But the cipher stone was stolen—and the keys with it!" Bess exclaimed.

"And what's more important, Dr. Pitt vanished at the same time. It is the fate of Joshua Pitt that's worrying me more than anything else. This morning I began to wonder if there might be some superstition about the Frog Treasure which the natives fear to discover themselves, and are afraid that we will discover. This might be a reason for holding him."

"Have you any idea what the superstition might be?" Nancy asked.

From an inner pocket Terry Scott pulled out a crude drawing. "I found this in Dr. Pitt's tent the next morning," he said.

It was actually three drawings in the form of a triangle; at the lower left, a frog; at the right, what appeared to be the prostrate figure of a man; and at the top of the triangle, a symbol representing the sun.

"What does it mean?" Bess asked.

Terry said he had not figured it out. But he was sure the riddle could be solved and Professor Pitt found.

"You see why I need the services of a fine lawyer, Mr. Drew," he said, "and also the help of a good detective like your daughter. Can't we start work at once?"

Carson Drew was thoughtful a moment. "It looks as if solving this mystery will have to be done in Mexico," he mused. Then, turning to his daughter, he said:

"I'm afraid, Nancy dear, that in this case you've started something you can't finish at this time—unless you go to Mexico. I can't spare you as far away from home as that, and besides, I have some work of my own for you to do for the next few days."

CHAPTER V

Suspicion

NANCY looked at her father in surprise, but she did not argue the point. She knew he would not have asked her to turn down Terry Scott's case without good reason.

The young man showed his disappointment, but he smiled politely. "Well, you can't blame me for trying, sir," he said, getting up from his chair. "Your daughter seemed to be the very person I needed to help me."

Nancy gave the mysterious drawing a last-minute look. "Have the other professors any idea what these signs mean?" she asked.

"No," Terry replied. "They haven't a glimmering. Well, I guess I'd better get back to my hotel."

"I must go, too," Bess added, rising.

As the two ambled along the elm-shaded avenue, Bess said, "Terry, I'm sorry about Nancy not being able to help you right now. Perhaps there'll be something she can do after she finishes her work for her father."

Terry looked hopeful. "Even if she can't go to Mexico?"

Bess laughed. "If you knew Nancy Drew as well as I do, you'd know she can't give up now. That brain of hers will keep on worrying and puzzling until she finds an answer. You'll see!"

While Bess was saying this, Nancy was on her way upstairs to her father's study. He had asked that they continue their conference up there.

"Dad, if I can't work on Terry's case," she said, "I should give back the half-key, don't you think?"

Mr. Drew decided this could wait; at least until he and his daughter finished the conference.

"Come here, my dear," he said. "I have something to show you."

He held up a large group photograph which bore the legend: *Hale College Geology Club*.

Nancy pounced on it delightedly. "Oh, there you are, Dad, in a funny-looking suit and cap. And whatever is that thing on your shoulder—a knapsack?"

"We were dressed for a field trip," her father explained. "Maybe you didn't know I studied geology when I was in college."

"I'm impressed, Dad," Nancy teased. "Is that solemn-looking man your professor?"

Carson Drew nodded. "I wondered if you'd ask about him. His name is Joshua Pitt."

Nancy stared. "*The* Joshua Pitt? The man on Terry Scott's expedition—the one who disappeared?"

"The same man," her father declared. "The fact is, Nancy, I not only studied under Professor Pitt when I was at Hale, but he and I eventually became good friends."

"I never heard you mention him until last night," Nancy said.

"I suppose not," her father agreed. "Dr. Pitt kept to himself a great deal. Never went visiting. He was unmarried and hadn't any relatives, and for the most part he avoided people socially. Yet he had a warmer heart than most men give him credit for."

"It sounds as if you know a great deal about him."

The lawyer smiled quizzically. "I know one thing Terry Scott may or may not know. And that's why I asked you not to continue trying to solve the mystery—at least until certain things can be proved."

Her father explained that Joshua Pitt's will left everything he owned to Terry Scott, and it was a nice sum of money.

"Dad! How did you learn that?"

"Because," he replied, "I drew up the will."

Nancy was astounded. Instantly she guessed what was in her father's mind. There was a chance Terry's whole story was a fake. The truth might be very ugly. For some reason best known to Terry, Dr. Pitt might never return and the young man would inherit the money!

"Oh, Dad, I just can't believe Terry's that kind of person," she cried out.

"Now don't get excited," her father said. "He probably isn't. But it's something to keep in mind."

Nancy nodded. "Why did he come to you for help, Dad? Did he tell you that?"

Mr. Drew crossed one leg over the other while he considered his answer. Finally he said:

"Terry quoted old Pitt as saying, 'If you're ever in trouble, go to Carson Drew. He'll get you out of it if anybody can.'"

"And you would," Nancy remarked loyally.

Her father made a mock bow. "Don't misunderstand. I like Terry, too. But my first interest is to protect Dr. Pitt. That's why I want you to take on a little research job."

Nancy leaned forward expectantly. That father of hers! He always had something up his sleeve. The mystery he had mentioned!

"I want you to go and see the other members of the expedition—Dr. Graham and Dr. Anderson," Mr. Drew proposed. "Find out what you can

about the expedition, and what they think of
Terry."

Nancy was eager to begin her work. "I'll start
with Dr. Graham. Terry says he's at Jonsonburg
College. Maybe George Fayne will drive over
there with me this afternoon."

Mr. Drew liked the idea, suggesting, however,
that she telephone Dr. Graham's office first and
arrange an appointment. The professor's secre-
tary answered Nancy's call and said that Dr.
Graham would talk with her at three fifteen.

Next Nancy telephoned George and asked if she
cared to accompany her to Jonsonburg College to
interview a professor. A snort came over the
wire.

"Hypers, Nancy, I don't know how to talk to a
doctor of—what is it? Archaeology! But I'll
go."

A few minutes before three fifteen, George and
Nancy were hurrying along the corridor of one
of the buildings at Jonsonburg College. They
stopped at a door marked Professor Graham, and
Nancy knocked.

A small, stooped man with beady eyes and
wrinkled, leathery cheeks opened the door. He
eyed the two girls briefly. When Nancy introduced herself and George, the professor looked
at his watch.

"I see you're punctual, Miss Drew. I like

young people to be on time." He stepped back from the door and invited them in.

Nancy told Dr. Graham that she was acquainted with Terry Scott, and through him had learned of the expedition to Mexico and the disappearance of Professor Pitt.

"My father is a friend of Professor Pitt and is much concerned about him," Nancy added. "He suggested that I come and talk to you."

The little man fixed his sharp, calculating eyes on the girl. "I suppose young Scott told you *he* found the cipher stone," he remarked coldly, ignoring the reference to Dr. Pitt.

"No," Nancy told him. "He said, 'Dr. Pitt and I.' Terry has a very high respect for your work, too, professor," she added hastily.

She could see the old man relax under this compliment. "Humph! He's an arrogant young fellow. But he has a good mind. I suppose you want my opinion of the case."

Nancy nodded.

"About Pitt, now." The old professor leaned back in his chair. "I don't mind saying his disappearance hardly surprised me. I like Pitt, but he's queer, secretive. He'll listen; he'll find out what others have on their minds, but he never will tell what he has found out. Why, he has written whole books he's put off publishing. My guess is he can't bear to let the world in on his secrets."

"Do you believe, Dr. Graham," Nancy spoke up, "that Dr. Pitt went off by himself to find the treasure?"

Graham shrugged. "It's possible. But one thing I don't believe; and that is that Pitt is in trouble. Everything was peaceful and quiet the night he left." Then he added, a half-smile on his face, "When it comes to that, some of us scientists are a bit selfish, not in acquiring money, but like boys collecting marbles. We want recognition, we want to discover things for ourselves. We're not always generous when we work together."

Suddenly the professor seemed to remember something, for his smile faded. "I'll give credit where credit is due," he said testily. "Terry Scott found that half-key and I agreed to let him take charge of it. But what does he know about keys? Nothing. I'm the one who knows."

With a jerk, the elderly man pulled a book from a shelf and displayed its title page: *Ancient Keys: Their History and Workmanship*, by Henry Graham, Ph.D.

"I wrote this book," he said, "when Terry Scott still was wearing rompers."

George stifled a giggle and Dr. Graham went on, "Now here's a key that would interest you girls. If you'd lived back in the days of Rome and were keeping house, this is what would unlock your front door."

He showed them a drawing of a key, which, he

said, was two feet long and might weigh as much as ten pounds.

"Hypers!" George grinned. "You'd need a suitcase to carry that around in!"

"You wouldn't have carried it," explained Dr. Graham. "This key was chained to a slave called the *janitor*, or doorkeeper, who in turn was chained to the door. His duty was to guard the door and the members of the household with his life."

"Quite a responsibility!" Nancy remarked with a grimace. "I didn't know that the word 'janitor' had such an interesting history. But speaking of keys, Dr. Graham, what do you think happened to the lost keys?"

The professor said he was working on an idea. He did not care to reveal it now. "But Terry will never be able to solve the mystery alone. He'll come back to me, wanting help."

"Have you any theories about the drawing he found in Dr. Pitt's tent?" Nancy asked.

Dr. Graham compressed his lips and shrugged. Did he know something he was not telling? Or was he too proud to admit that he could not explain the secret message?

Nancy knew it would be difficult to find out whether or not he had any suspicion about Terry in connection with Dr. Pitt's disappearance. At last she broached the subject. Dr. Graham stood up dramatically and pounded his desk.

"The idea!" he stormed when he got the full import of her question. "Maybe we four did have our differences about what we ought to do on that expedition, but I want to tell you this: not one of us would harm another for all the treasure in Mexico!"

"That's just what I wanted to hear," Nancy said, rising. "And thank you for letting me come."

Very much relieved, she and George left Dr. Graham's office. Terry Scott's name had been cleared!

On the way home George kept eying Nancy, who did little talking. Instead, she hummed various popular tunes, a continuous smile on her face as she drove.

"Ned Nickerson," George suggested with a sly grin, "will be surprised when he learns about your interest in professors. When are you seeing him again?"

Nancy grinned back. "This week end."

After supper that evening Ned telephoned from his fraternity house, Omega Chi Epsilon, at Emerson.

"You're not forgetting our date this week end?" he asked anxiously. "I thought you'd write."

"Of course I haven't forgotten, Ned," Nancy assured him. "I've a marvelous memory for dates—when they're for house parties at Emerson."

"Before I forget, I have a favor to ask, Nancy. There's a long-haired professor visiting River Heights—a fraternity brother of mine. He needs a lift to Emerson."

Nancy laughed. "Why, Ned, are you asking me to drive over with another man?"

Ned snorted. "That old codger? He's probably sixty if he's a day. He's due to give a lecture here, and you know those week-end trains. I thought you wouldn't mind bringing him with you Friday."

"Glad to."

"By the way," Ned added, "ask him to bring his fabulous frog along."

"What?"

"Frog. According to an article he wrote, he has an ancient jade frog. Supposed to be quite interesting."

Another professor interested in ancient frogs!

Nancy wondered if this could have anything to do with the mystery she was trying to solve. Perhaps this might even be the frog Terry was seeking!

"All right," Nancy said. "I'll bring the man and his frog. Where's he staying?"

"At the Claymore. And one more little detail," Ned added, as Nancy tried to conceal her excitement, "the professor's name is Terence Scott."

CHAPTER VI

The Highway Trap

TERRY!

Nancy gasped in surprise and amusement. The situation was funny, but it might have a sinister side, too.

Had Terry found the Frog Treasure but was not admitting it? Was he trying to hide the fact that he had opened it with the obsidian keys and removed the treasure? No one would be the wiser!

"What's the matter?" Ned asked, as Nancy hesitated in her reply. "You're not backing down, are you? The old professor's probably not a bad sort."

"Oh, no," Nancy assured him. She was tempted to reveal Terry's age but decided the joke was too good to spoil. "I'm sure Professor Scott will be very pleasant company," she added. "See you Friday, Ned. 'Bye now!"

She put down the telephone, and burst out

laughing. As she entered the living room, still laughing, her father said:

"When you can talk again, tell me the joke. I'm curious."

Between outbursts of giggles, Nancy told him Ned's remark about the "long-haired, sixty-year-old" Terry Scott. Mr. Drew joined in the hilarity. Then, sobering, Nancy told about the frog.

"Dad, you remember what Terry said about the treasure he was seeking? Could that be the frog Ned wants him to bring?"

"If you really want to know, why don't you ask Terry Scott?" Carson Drew advised.

"I'll phone him this minute," cried Nancy.

Her father shook his head. "Why don't we drive around to his hotel together?" he suggested. "We can watch his reactions to our questions."

Ten minutes later the lawyer and his daughter were being welcomed by the young scientist in his room at the Claymore.

"So glad you came over," he said. "I hope it means you've changed your mind about taking my case."

"Not yet," Mr. Drew said. "But my detective daughter has a question or two she would like you to answer."

"First of all," Nancy said, her eyes twinkling, "I've been commissioned to issue an invitation to an elderly professor—about sixty years old. His name, I am told, is Terence Scott."

Terry looked perplexed until Nancy told him about Ned's telephone call. The young professor laughed loudly at the joke. He said he would be delighted to drive to Emerson with her on Friday.

"But is that the question you came to ask me? I thought for a minute you were going to quiz me about the Mexican mystery."

"I am," Nancy admitted. "Ned told me you have a valuable jade frog, and he wants you to bring it along."

She watched Terry's face as he got ready to answer. Certainly there was no sign of guilt on it.

"Oh, that!" Terry laughed. "I suppose your friend means the frog I *had*. I sold it. It was a beauty, too. Fine old jade. The workmanship was similar to Oriental pieces I've seen."

"You found it in Mexico?"

"I bought it there. That frog meant a lot to me, because it was pretty strong support for a theory I'm trying to prove."

"What is it?" Mr. Drew asked.

"Well, to begin with, that jade frog I bought wasn't merely old. It was positively ancient. It was carved during a period so far back in human history that very little is known about it."

The young man spoke eagerly. "Some scientists believe that during a certain period in history, tribes from Asia traveled to America by way of a strip of land that connected Asia with what's now Alaska. Later the land disappeared into the ocean. Their descendants wandered south, some of them settling in Mexico."

"What a fascinating theory!" Nancy exclaimed.

"Why did you sell the frog?" Mr. Drew spoke up.

Terry smiled. He said the curator of a museum had told him he wanted to buy the valuable piece from him; that it belonged in a place where many people could see it.

"Finally, he convinced me," Terry concluded.

Mr. Drew arose. "Terry," he said, "Nancy and I thought maybe we'd see the frog."

Before leaving, Nancy spoke of the obsidian half-key, saying that perhaps she should have brought it along. Terry begged her to keep it.

"I haven't given up hope you'll agree to help me solve the mystery," he said, smiling. "Anyway, I wouldn't want to leave the key here while I'm gone, and there's no reason for taking it to Emerson."

Outside the hotel, Mr. Drew confided to Nancy that he was fast losing any suspicion he might have had regarding Terry, but there were still points about Dr. Pitt's disappearance which needed explaining.

"Maybe I'll learn more over the week end," Nancy said hopefully. "I'll call on Dr. Anderson. He's not far from Emerson."

Next day she busied herself with preparations for the week-end party. She bought a new aqua evening dress, which George said was too fussy but which Bess called "dreamy." Then, after purchasing slippers to match and a few accessories, Nancy was ready.

Friday was a warm, sunny day. Nancy decided to put down the top of her convertible. Promptly at eleven o'clock she pulled up in front of the professor's hotel. He was waiting.

Soon they were rolling along the fine highway toward Emerson College. Terry complimented Nancy on her efficient driving. It was not long before they found themselves once more discussing the mystery in Mexico.

"You've never told me much about Juarez Tino," Nancy said. "I'd like to hear more about him."

"That's rather a long story," Terry answered. "Mind if I tell it while we're eating? I'm starved."

Nancy admitted that she, too, was ready to eat. She parked her car at an attractive roadside restaurant, near the brow of a hill, and they found a secluded corner.

"I disliked Juarez Tino," Terry told her, "the first day I saw him. He was a slippery, shifty sort of fellow. According to his story, he was exploring a neighboring site. But he was always coming over to see what we were doing.

"He asked hundreds of questions, and prowled around our excavation ditches after dark to see if we'd left anything around. I was sure he was up to some deviltry."

"Did the other professors distrust him, too?"

"They didn't suspect him in the same way I did. Dr. Pitt told me to ignore the fellow. I didn't agree. It seemed to me that if we let Juarez hang around, sooner or later we'd have trouble on our hands."

"Did you?"

"One day I lost my temper. I told Juarez to keep out of our excavation. We had a regular set-to, and the upshot was that I ran him off the place."

"Did you find out anything about him?"

"Nothing very conclusive. He'd taken a few courses somewhere and had a smattering of this and that. His specialty was supposed to be ancient gems. But his reputation wasn't good. The story went around that he'd once tried to pass off some fake pieces."

Nancy asked if Juarez had ever come back after he was chased away.

"Yes. Although he stayed out of my sight, he did plenty of snooping when he thought I wasn't around. Once in a while I would get a glimpse of his wife."

"What was she like?"

The young man frowned. "You wouldn't like

her, Nancy. She wears loud clothes and always makes herself conspicuous. She has a bold manner, and her voice is harsh. In fact, her whole personality suggested just one thing to me—cruelty."

Nancy's imagination had started working. This couple sounded like a perfect pair to do almost any underhanded work. No doubt they could tell something about Dr. Pitt, if they would.

"I guess we'd better leave," Terry said, bringing Nancy back to reality. "We'll have to hurry if we're to reach Emerson in time for dinner."

"Yes," she replied, in a somewhat absent tone of voice.

As she and Terry stepped outdoors into the sunshine, she was not thinking of the dinner party at Emerson. She was thinking of cruel Mrs. Juarez Tino and her shifty husband. If Professor Pitt were in their clutches, things would not go well with him, she felt sure.

Nancy was about to step into her car when Terry touched her arm. "Look!" he said in a low, tense voice. "Those two men up the hill— they're watching us."

When Nancy turned her head to look, the pair, with hats pulled low over their faces, stepped hurriedly into a black sedan. The car quickly got under way and passed out of sight over the top of the hill.

"They ran the minute we looked at them,"

said Terry. "I wonder why they did that."

"Did you recognize them?" Nancy asked.

"No."

"We'll watch out for them, just the same," Nancy decided.

"I'll feel better when we get to Emerson," Terry replied a bit nervously. "Perhaps you'd better speed up."

Nancy shook off her somber mood and grinned mischievously. "Do you suppose your elderly nerves can stand the strain, professor?"

"Give them a try, Miss Drew!"

They stepped into her car and she started it rolling once more toward Emerson. Guiding the wheel expertly, Nancy watched the speedometer creep steadily higher. They did not overtake the two sinister-looking strangers in the black car. Finally, she and Terry began to enjoy the flying landscape, the swift rush of wind, the dips and curves of the road.

Then suddenly—too late—they saw disaster ahead. As they rounded a bend, they saw the wide repair ditch. Desperately Nancy wrenched the wheel to the left.

But she could not make it in time. There was a hurtling impact as the car nose-dived into the ditch!

CHAPTER VII

The Professor's Secret

WHEN Nancy regained consciousness a few minutes later, she was lying in soft, soggy grass at the side of the road. Terry Scott was bending over her.

"Nancy!" he whispered anxiously. "Are you—"

"I'm all right. Really I am," she managed to say, but her head ached badly. "You're not hurt?"

"A few bruises. It's lucky we landed in this soft spot."

The couple surveyed the car ruefully. It lay on one side like some giant, grotesque bug.

"There should have been a road-block sign," Nancy said grimly.

Terry pointed. "There was a sign—but not where it should have been."

Lying at the side of the ditch was a long board. "Danger. Road Repairs. Drive Slowly," he read aloud. "A lot of good that does us now! The road gang shouldn't have been so careless."

"Don't blame the road gang," Nancy said. "I believe that sign was deliberately removed just before we got here. Otherwise, somebody else would have hit the ditch ahead of us."

"Nancy, that would be murder!"

"It very nearly was murder," she answered. "And by those two men who were watching us at the restaurant, I'll bet."

Terry dragged the sign around the bend to warn other motorists. He had just returned to Nancy when they heard the squeal of brakes. The couple were worried. Maybe those same men—

Nancy and Terry relaxed as they saw a kindly-looking, middle-aged couple in the car that came around the bend.

"Oh, my dears!" the woman cried, getting out of the car. "Is anyone—"

Terry said no one else was involved in the accident. Nancy added that they were all right except for her headache.

The woman took a tiny bottle from her purse, and held it to Nancy's nose. The strong whiff of smelling salts cleared the girl's head instantly.

"Oh, thank you," she said.

The man offered the young people a ride, but they preferred waiting until a wrecker could come. The friendly strangers promised to stop at the next town and send back mechanics, as well as a state trooper.

A few minutes later a wrecking car arrived and two men in overalls stepped out.

"Whew!" one whistled. "I'd say you folks are lucky you didn't get killed."

In a short time they had Nancy's car right side up and were checking the engine, chassis, and wheels for possible damage.

Both mechanics grinned. "Some car!" one commented. "She's got a few dents and scratches. But no real harm done by her tumble. No reason why you two can't keep goin' under your own power. 'Course, you'd better check again when you get where you're goin'."

As they were leaving, a state trooper rode up on a motorcycle. Nancy and Terry told him their story. He said that a watch would be set for the two men whom the young people thought were responsible for the removal of the road sign. When asked for a reason, Terry owned up that he thought he had an enemy and mentioned the attack on him at the hotel.

The trooper promised to make a full report. Then Nancy and Terry started off once more for Emerson. Terry took the wheel.

"You relax and pamper that head of yours," he told Nancy, "or you won't be able to show up at the dance tomorrow. I'm counting on at least one dance with you, young lady."

"Are you going?" Nancy asked in surprise.

"Well, that depends on whether or not I get an invitation."

"I'll be looking for you," Nancy said.

When they reached Emerson College, Terry got off at the president's home, where he had been invited to stay as a week-end guest. Nancy drove on to the Omega Chi Epsilon house to meet Ned Nickerson.

Tall, athletic Ned saw Nancy drive up and ran out to greet her. When he noticed the dents in the car and Nancy's disheveled appearance, he gasped:

"What happened? Were you in an accident?"

After she told what had occurred, Ned's tanned face took on a look of deep concern. He insisted she go at once to the college infirmary for a check up, and drove her there. To his relief she was pronounced all right.

On the way back to the fraternity house, Ned asked whether Professor Scott had come with her.

"Yes, and he wasn't hurt in the accident."

"I'm glad the poor old man didn't break any bones," Ned said sympathetically, and Nancy had all she could do to keep from laughing. "By the way," Ned went on, "how did you and the prof hit it off? Was he much bother?"

Nancy smiled demurely. "He was a lamb. He even insisted on driving part of the way himself."

Ned laughed appreciatively. "I can just see him at the wheel!"

"And you know what I think you should do, Ned? Invite him to the fraternity dance."

Ned looked incredulous. "What! An old fossil like Dr. Scott?"

"Well, why not?" Nancy challenged. "As your fraternity brother, he'd be immensely flattered. And who knows? He might even be a good dancer."

"All right," Ned agreed reluctantly. "I'll see that he gets an invitation. But don't blame me if he doesn't enjoy the party."

Nancy laughed. "I'll take my chance on that."

At supper she mentioned that her father wished her to call on Dr. Anderson, a professor of geology at Clifton Institute near by.

"It would be nice if you could drive me over," she said. "How about Sunday, right after chapel?"

Ned agreed, at the same time noticing the look of secrecy on Nancy's face. He put down his dessertspoon.

"Look here, Nancy. Is this some more of your detective work?"

Nancy admitted that she had become interested in a fascinating mystery and would tell him more about it on the drive over. For the time being she was just going to enjoy the house party.

Next afternoon was Emerson's first big football game of the season. It was a close contest with Harper, Emerson pulling ahead only in the last quarter to win by a score of 14 to 7.

Ned played a spectacular game at quarterback. He scored the first touchdown on a brilliant dash around the Harper end, and threw a pass to the left halfback for the winning touchdown. Nancy cheered until her voice began to sound like the croaking of a frog.

Later, when the fraternity dance was about to begin, Nancy was called to the telephone. Her worried father said he had just heard of the accident and was anxious to know if she was all right.

"Oh, yes. Don't worry," his daughter said reassuringly, and told him of the wonderful time she was having.

As she and Ned began to dance, he remarked that he had not seen any elderly men. "I guess Professor Scott decided not to come."

A few minutes later Nancy saw a tall young man, in immaculate evening attire, on the fringe of the crowd. As she and Ned reached him, she stopped and said:

"Hello! I'm glad you got here. Ned, I'd like you to meet Professor Terence Scott. Terry, this is your fraternity brother Ned Nickerson."

Terry put out his hand. Ned's jaw dropped and he gave Nancy a sidewise glance, as the name Scott hit him like a delayed-action bomb.

"You're Professor Scott who's giving a lecture here tomorrow?"

Terry grinned. "I guess I am, Brother Nickerson!"

Ned shot Nancy an "I'll-get-even" look, then burst out laughing. "Well, you two kept your secret well," he said.

He immediately introduced Terry to his fraternity brothers and the girls with them, and told them about the joke on himself. Terry became popular at once, and when the dance ended, he told Nancy and Ned he had not had so much fun since his own college days.

Directly after chapel service next day, Nancy and Ned set out for Clifton Institute.

Nancy kept her promise to tell Ned about the mystery of the black key, and the strange events that had taken place in connection with it.

"That's why I want to talk to Dr. Anderson," she concluded. "I want to find out what he knows. He may give us a clue."

They located the robust, forty-five-year-old professor sitting in a garden behind one of the faculty houses, though the day had turned cold. He wore comfortable tweeds and was puffing on a briar pipe.

"Never find me indoors, weather like this," he told his callers after Nancy had introduced herself and Ned. "As a matter of fact, I don't believe in indoor classrooms."

Dr. Anderson went on to explain that he could teach his students more on field trips than they could possibly get out of books. "They'll learn more facts and have more fun besides."

Here was an unusual man, Nancy and Ned decided. "Do you conduct your Clifton Institute classes outdoors, sir?" Ned asked.

The man nodded. "Our president and I, fortunately, see eye to eye on that idea. This fall, for instance, I'm taking a group of special students from various colleges on a field trip to Florida."

"How exciting!" exclaimed Nancy, and Ned said he wished he could go along.

"Great country, Florida," the professor said. "Fascinating history."

Nancy maneuvered the conversation to Mexico, and explained that her father knew Dr. Joshua Pitt. Did Dr. Anderson have any theories about where Pitt might be?

The question seemed to annoy the professor. With a frown, he replied, "I'm interested in facts, not theories, Miss Drew."

He further astounded her by saying that Juarez Tino had called on him a few weeks before, and had offered to produce Pitt and the missing cipher tablet if Anderson would pay him a good sum of money.

"You didn't do it?" Nancy asked excitedly.

"That rascally scoundrel?" exploded the professor. "I should say not. I threw him out of my office!"

"Then you don't think he knows where Dr. Pitt is?" Nancy questioned.

"I don't know. I'm beginning to wonder if I was too hasty in throwing him out."

Nancy asked a few more questions, but Dr. Anderson seemed to become evasive. Knowing she could get no more information from him, Nancy thanked him for the interview and left with Ned. As they drove back to Emerson, Nancy remarked:

"If I had been in Dr. Anderson's place, I would have tried to find out where Juarez Tino went."

Ned agreed. "Do you suppose he really captured Dr. Pitt for ransom?"

"If he did, there's no telling what might happen to the poor man," Nancy said. "I must find Juarez Tino just as soon as I can!"

"Sounds too dangerous," Ned retorted. "Remember, I want you all in one piece for the winter prom!"

"Don't worry," Nancy replied. "I hope the mystery will be solved long before then."

That afternoon she and Ned attended Terry Scott's lecture at the college auditorium. The young scientist thrilled his audience with a story about a certain Mexican jungle where there had once lived an ancient race of people quite unlike any of their neighbors. From statues that had been found it was thought they might have been pygmies.

"But they were people of a high culture," Terry said, "who made many beautiful objects. These are just beginning to be uncovered. I had some colored pictures of them, but unfortunately all of my slides, as well as my notes, mysteriously disappeared a short time ago."

Nancy whispered to Ned that this was when Terry was assaulted at his hotel. Toward the end of the lecture the young professor mentioned his own work in Mexico and the cipher stone.

"Some day I hope to come back here and tell you that the cipher stone has solved a great mystery," he remarked, looking straight at Nancy.

When the lecture was over, his listeners applauded loudly.

"Never heard people so enthusiastic over this kind of lecture," Ned declared as he and Nancy left the auditorium.

"Terry's really good, isn't he?" Nancy asked. Then she added impulsively, "Oh, I do hope he'll discover that ancient secret!"

"Speaking of secrets," Ned said, "you've been here two days and you still haven't given me an invitation."

"To what?"

Ned Nickerson groaned. "The Young Colony Ball you girls are giving Thanksgiving Eve at the

River Heights Yacht Club.   Miss Drew, are you going to invite me to that dance, or aren't you?"

Nancy looked at him in astonishment, then blushed. "Honestly, Ned, I'd forgotten all about it. But I'll invite you, of course—if I go."

"*If* you go? Do you mean there's a chance of your not going?"

"To tell the truth, Ned, I may be up to my eyebrows by that time in the study of ancient stones."

"In one of Terry Scott's courses, I suppose," Ned remarked with conspicuous lack of enthusiasm.

"No. In Florida."

CHAPTER VIII

The Warning

"WELL, I'm glad you're back, and safe and sound," said Hannah Gruen as she met Nancy at the door Monday afternoon. "I still shiver when I think of your car turning over!"

"How did you learn of it?" Nancy asked. "I didn't think to ask Dad when he called."

"It was in Saturday night's paper."

Nancy was sorry to hear this. The men she suspected now would know that their scheme had worked—in some measure, at least.

"Any news here?" Nancy asked.

"Yes. Your father left town. Didn't say when he'd be back. And call Bess or George right away."

"Important?"

"If you could hear them, you'd think so! They tried to get in touch with you at Emerson but couldn't reach you."

Nancy hurried to the telephone and called the Marvin house.

"At last!" Bess gasped. "Wait there. George and I will be right over."

A few minutes later the cousins arrived in the Marvin car. They joined Nancy in her bedroom where she was unpacking.

"Did you have fun? How'd the joke about Terry turn out?" Bess began.

George cut her short. "Let's tell Nancy our news first. She might want to report it to the police."

"Yes, please do," Nancy begged, her interest thoroughly awakened.

The girls said they might have a clue to the person or persons who had caused the car accident.

"It all started in Cliffwood," said Bess. "Remember that terrible man who said all those awful things to you at the airport?"

"You mean Wilfred Porterly?"

"He's the one," George took up the story. "Bess and I were shopping at Carson's in Cliffwood Friday. We stopped at the necktie counter to buy my dad a birthday present, and there was Porterly buying himself a hand-painted tie."

Bess giggled. "He was too busy admiring himself to notice us. George and I scooted to the next aisle and watched him."

The cousins were so sure he had not been telling the truth about himself at the airport that they had decided to follow him and see what they could find out.

"We trailed him to a hotel, where he went into a phone booth," George reported. "He dialed a number and talked to somebody named King."

"Conway King?" Nancy asked excitedly.

"I don't know. He just said King. But he was talking about you, Nancy. We heard him say, 'That Drew girl and Scott are acting too smart. You know what to do.' "

"Then what happened?"

"King must have answered quickly and to the point, because Porterly said, 'That sounds all right.' Then he hung up."

Bess said the girls had expected Porterly to go upstairs, and were just planning what to do next, when he suddenly went downstairs and out a rear entrance.

"We followed him," said George, "but he disappeared. I think he caught a glimpse of us."

"The hotel clerk said nobody was registered there under the name of Porterly," Bess added.

"Was there a Mr. King listed?" Nancy asked.

"No," George replied. "We're sure he's the one who caused the accident."

"You're probably right," Nancy agreed grimly. "What time did Porterly make the phone call?"

"A little after ten," George declared. "It must have been, because we left home at nine."

Nancy was thoughtful as she laid a sweater in a

lower bureau drawer. How long would it have taken Porterly to drive from the hotel in Cliffwood to the spot along the highway where she and Terry had seen the two men? Two hours at the most, she decided. She and Terry had stopped at the restaurant about twelve o'clock.

It was too bad she had got only a brief glimpse of the men's backs as they had stepped hurriedly into the parked sedan. Had the shorter one been King—in other words, Juarez Tino back from Florida? Had the taller man been Porterly, or another friend?

Nancy told her friends about the two strangers who had been watching the restaurant.

"Nancy, you might have been killed!" Bess said with a shiver.

George agreed. "Why don't you leave town for a while?" she suggested. "Those villains are plotting trouble for you as well as for Terry. Since one plan didn't work, they'll try another."

"I'll tell you what, Nancy," said Bess. "Come over to my house and stay until your father gets home. I can't bear to think of your being in this big house without him."

"Don't worry," Nancy protested. "Hannah Gruen is my bulwark and defender. Remember the other night?"

Bess said no more about it, but excused herself, saying she wanted to talk to Hannah. A few minutes later Nancy and George could hear cupboard doors being opened and closed. There was a clash of pans and utensils.

George grinned. "Bess and that appetite of hers! I'll bet she persuaded Hannah to make her one of those utterly devilish chocolate cakes."

"Sounds like it," Nancy agreed with a smile.

But she was not really thinking of her friend's appetite. She was remembering what George had told her about Porterly's message to King. "*Scott and that Drew girl are acting too smart. You know what to do—*"

She ought to warn Terry!

Telling George what she had in mind, Nancy hurried into her father's room and picked up the telephone. But she was not able to reach Terry at his hotel. At six o'clock, however, he called her back. Nancy quickly related the story and her suspicions.

Terry whistled in surprise. "Well, that clears up the mystery of the road sign," he remarked.

"When they find their scheme didn't work," Nancy said, "they'll try something else. Terry, you're the one they're really after. I think you should leave town for a few days. Stay out of sight."

"Oh, I'll be all right," the young professor replied reassuringly. "But how about you? Does your father know what happened?"

Nancy told him that her father was away for an indefinite stay.

"That settles it," Terry said. "You and Mrs. Gruen should not be in that house tonight. Stay at some hotel."

"Nonsense," Nancy told him. "We'll be perfectly safe, especially if Juarez Tino thinks I'm scared off the case. But why do you have to stay in River Heights?"

"I have no choice. You know I'm a bit of a linguist. A woman here in River Heights engaged me just this afternoon to translate an old diary for her, and I've accepted. It belonged to her grandfather, a sea captain. It's sort of a puzzle and she has persuaded me to decipher it for her."

"Can't you do your translating somewhere else, while you're in hiding?" Nancy asked.

Terry said the woman considered the diary a priceless relic and would not permit it out of her sight. That meant he would have to work on it at her home in River Heights.

"But here's an idea," he said. "She and her husband have invited me to stay with them while I'm doing the work."

"Well, that might be safer than staying at the hotel," Nancy said. "I'd suggest you go there immediately. But please do it quietly. Don't let Juarez Tino or Porterly know where you are!"

"All right," Terry agreed. "If you want to get in touch with me, I'll be at the Earl Wangells'. They're in the phone book."

A sudden look of alarm came into Nancy's eyes. "Terry, did you say the Wangells? On Fairview Avenue?"

"Yes. Do you know them?"

Nancy's voice was excited now. "Terry, listen to me. I don't know the Wangells personally. But I know about them. And I beg you, don't go there and stay. Don't even take the job!"

Terry was astounded.

"Why not?" he asked.

"I can't tell you over the phone. But Dad would say the same thing if he were here. Please don't go there, Terry."

For a minute he did not reply. When he did speak, the young man's voice was kindly but determined.

"Thanks for warning me. But I've just got to run the risk. I must see that diary again," he said. "I believe it will help solve the mystery of the black keys."

CHAPTER IX

A Mysterious Diary

CONFLICTING thoughts raced through Nancy's mind. Her father distrusted the Wangells. Why had they contacted Terry? And why did he think the diary would aid in solving the mystery of the black keys?

"Please," she said, "let's talk about this some more before you go to the Wangells' again. But not on the phone or at my house. I'm having supper at George Fayne's. Could you come there afterward?"

Terry agreed. At eight o'clock he arrived. After introducing him to George's parents, Nancy excused herself and led Terry to the sunroom.

"The first thing I want to know," the young professor said, once he was seated, "is why you distrust the Wangells."

"A friend of Dad's," Nancy replied, "handled a case in which the Wangells were involved. Did you ever hear of the Clancy swindle?"

"No."

Nancy explained that several years before, the Wangells had done some traveling in Europe. When they came back, they had set themselves up as experts on rare, old pictures. They sold them privately to wealthy people.

"Fake art dealers?" Terry suggested.

"Yes. They convinced a widow named Mrs. Clancy they had some rare French paintings. She paid the Wangells a fancy price for them, only to discover later that the pictures were worthless."

"Did she sue?" Terry asked.

"Yes. But the Wangells played innocent. They claimed they had bought the pictures from a young man named DuPlaine, and had been duped themselves—that DuPlaine had painted the pictures and forged the famous artist's signature."

"How did you hear of the case?" Terry wanted to know.

"A friend of Dad's was called in to defend DuPlaine," Nancy replied. "DuPlaine admitted he painted the pictures but said they were only copies he had made, as a student, in the museums. He had sold them as copies for practically nothing."

"What was the Wangells' answer to that?"

"They acted injured and indignant. Mr. Wangell had a bill of sale and all sorts of documents to prove they had paid a high price."

Terry asked how the case had been settled. Nancy said the court had decided there was insufficient evidence, and dismissed the case.

"But my father always believed that the Wangells had forged the bill of sale, the documents, and the signatures on the paintings."

"Nice people," Terry commented.

"You see why I'm convinced they're up to something dishonest in this diary business," Nancy said. "It seems odd that Mrs. Wangell won't let you borrow it."

"She says she can't run the risk of losing it," Terry replied.

"I wonder if that's the real reason," Nancy mused. "And by the way, you haven't told me what Mrs. Wangell's diary has to do with the mystery of the black keys."

"Just this. Certain legends we professors came across, and some scientific data which seemed to prove they were true, led us to make the expedition in the first place. From skimming through the diary, I could see it is full of unpublished legends which I suspect might have some bearing on our case."

"How?"

"Mrs. Wangell's sea-captain grandfather retired in Florida, but he'd picked up stories everywhere, especially in Mexico."

"I see why you want to read the diary." Nancy smiled. "But I still don't like your dealing with the Wangells. Promise you won't stay there. How about going to a small hotel tonight and sending for your baggage so no one will know where you are?"

"I'd like to please you," Terry replied. "And be safe besides." He grinned. "I'll go from here to the Parkview and ask a porter to bring my things over there. Ever since that attack, I've kept everything locked in my bags, so the move will be easy."

At this moment George came in, wanting to know whether the conference was over. Nancy brought her up to date on the mystery, adding:

"Do you know where that Mrs. Wangell on Fairview Avenue came from?"

George grimaced. "You mean that fake art dealer's wife? I sure do. Right across the river. Her name was Lillian Webster. She tried to pretend she was quite somebody after she married, but our laundress told me she was awfully dumb in school."

Nancy asked if George knew anything about Mrs. Wangell's grandfather, but she said no. Why?

"I believe we ought to check the story of his being a sea captain and the valuable diary belonging to him," Nancy said.

Terry lifted his eyebrows. "I never thought of that. It would be a smart idea."

Nancy turned to George. "I'm sorry, George.

I haven't been the least bit sociable since supper, and now I know you'll think I'm rude. But would you mind terribly if Terry and I go now? I want to stop at Mrs. Prescott's on the way home."

George groaned. "Hypers, Nancy, I thought we could have a little music after your talk." She added with a mischievous grin, "Terry has never heard you play!"

"This is important, really it is," Nancy replied, begging off. "We ought to find out about Mrs. Wangell's grandfather before Terry goes back there."

As he and Nancy drove to Mrs. Prescott's, Nancy explained that the woman's business was tracing family trees.

"She has studied the history of every family in this area. She's president of the local historical society and has stacks of records."

Mrs. Prescott was at home in her expansive Victorian home and welcomed her guests at once into the library. She seemed delighted to have Nancy ask a question on her favorite subject.

"Mrs. Wangell? Let me see," she mused, squeezing her pince-nez glasses onto her nose. "You say she was Lillian Webster before she married?"

The woman's eyes studied the shelves. "This will take a little while, my dear. Do you mind waiting?"

"Not at all," Nancy replied.

When at last Mrs. Prescott turned away from her books and records, and took off her glasses, Nancy and Terry exchanged glances. Mrs. Prescott was frowning.

"I have checked both of Mrs. Wangell's grandfathers," she said, "and neither of them was a sea captain."

Nancy pretended surprise.

"It's all in the record," Mrs. Prescott insisted. "Isaac Webster, in the paternal line, was a farmer all his life. Her mother's father, Amos Groff, was a carpenter. Neither of them followed the sea at any time."

"I guess I have the story confused," Nancy murmured.

She thanked Mrs. Prescott for her help and hurried out to the car with Terry.

"You see, Mrs. Wangell isn't to be trusted," Nancy said. "I think you should insist upon taking that diary to the hotel and translating it before she becomes suspicious and changes her mind."

"She'll never agree to my taking it," Terry objected.

Nancy thought a moment. Suddenly she remembered a tiny camera her father had given her on her latest birthday. She kept it in the compartment of her car. Now she took it out and gave it to Terry.

"Put this in your pocket and take it to the Wangells' tomorrow. It's all set with self-developing film. Ask to borrow the diary—and if Mrs. Wangell refuses, take pictures of the pages you think may be especially important."

Terry promised to do as she suggested. Then, making sure they were not being followed, Nancy drove him to his new hotel, the Parkview.

"Sure you'll be all right?" he asked. "I hate to think of your going home alone and spending the night in that big house without your father."

"Nonsense! I'm not the least bit worried," Nancy said with a laugh.

"Just the same, I'm going to phone you in twenty minutes to be sure you're there," the young man declared.

Though Nancy was not alarmed over the situation, it was quite apparent, when she reached home, that Hannah Gruen was. The faithful housekeeper was waiting at the front door, her face pale and tense.

"Thank goodness you're back!" she exclaimed. "I phoned Mrs. Fayne and she said you had left quite a while ago. I didn't know what to think."

Nancy put an affectionate hand on the woman's shoulder. "You're a lamb to be so concerned. But here I am, safe and sound. And maybe tomorrow Dad will come home."

As Nancy started upstairs, the telephone rang. The housekeeper jumped in alarm.

"Don't be frightened," Nancy said. "I'm sure it's Terry."

Even Hannah could hear the relief in his voice as Nancy answered.

"And now do get some sleep," the housekeeper said solicitously when Nancy finished her telephone conversation. "You lost plenty of it this week end."

"Aren't you coming up?" Nancy asked as the housekeeper walked into the living room.

"I'll be up after a while—still some chores to do," she replied.

Nancy knew there was no use arguing, when Mrs. Gruen spoke with such determination. She went up to her room, undressed, and slid into bed. As she dropped off to sleep, she could hear the distant clatter of Hannah busying herself in the kitchen.

"I wonder if she made Bess that chocolate cake," Nancy thought sleepily. Then her eyes closed.

When she opened them again, it was in bewildered alarm. Somewhere in the darkened house there was a loud banging and jangling.

Simultaneously something crashed heavily and there was the thud of footsteps.

CHAPTER X

The Strange Numbers

SPRINGING out of bed, Nancy threw a robe around her and rushed into the hall. There was no further sound. The entire house was in darkness.

Her first thought was of Hannah Gruen. Stepping quickly into the housekeeper's bedroom, she flicked on the light. The room was empty, the bed not turned down.

Suddenly Nancy heard a moan from the floor below. Reaching the head of the stairs, she turned on the lower hall light.

Near the front door lay Hannah Gruen! Beyond her right hand, where she had evidently dropped it, was a rolling pin. Stretched across the hall between a radiator and a chair was a homemade burglar alarm—clothesline strung with tin pans and kitchen utensils. Nancy raced down.

"Hannah!" she cried, bending over the housekeeper. "What happened?"

The plucky woman opened her eyes and whispered, "Get him! Get him!"

Nancy looked out the hall window but saw no one. She helped the housekeeper to a couch, then raced through the first floor, peering into closets and behind doors. There was no sign of any disturbance except in the hall. Evidently the burglar alarm had scared off the intruder.

Nancy notified the police. Then she hurried back to Hannah.

"Shall I call a doctor?" she asked anxiously.

The woman shook her head. "I don't want anybody fussing over me. All I've got is bruises —and a bump on my head."

"Did he hit you with something?"

"No. I heard him trying to open the front door lock, so I waited in the dark. I thought if he got in, he'd run into that line, and I'd nab him. But I wasn't quick enough. When he hit those pans, one of them caught me on the head and dazed me a bit. That's why I didn't see where he went."

Nancy brought a washcloth wrung out in ice water and bathed Mrs. Gruen's swollen forehead.

"My, that feels good," the housekeeper said.

Nancy asked why the strange burglar alarm had been put up. She knew Hannah had some information she was not telling.

"I had an idea someone might visit us," the woman confessed, and said she had rigged an alarm at each door and window on the first floor.

She put a hand in her apron pocket and pulled out a note. The words were printed boldly in pencil and there was no signature. The message read:

NO MORE INTERFERENCE OR THERE WILL BE
TROUBLE FOR YOU

"Where did you find this?" Nancy asked quickly.

"Somebody slipped it under the kitchen door. I found it this morning when I went out to get the milk."

"I wonder who the 'you' is intended to be," Nancy mused.

"It's meant for you, Nancy. It's on account of that case you're working on for Professor Scott."

Nancy thought so, too. She believed the note might have been written by Juarez Tino. But she did not wish to alarm Mrs. Gruen.

"It may not be for me at all," she said soothingly. "Dad makes enemies in his law work, you know. It may be from someone like that."

Hannah started to speak, but Nancy patted her arm and continued, "You were a darling—and brave, too—to rig up that burglar alarm and lie in wait. You almost caught him!"

"Oh, that was Bess's idea," Hannah said, smiling weakly. "She thought we should do something to protect you."

"You're both dears," Nancy exclaimed, re-membering the clatter when Mrs. Gruen and Bess had been together in the kitchen. "And all the time I thought you were making Bess a chocolate cake!" she said, laughing.

Just then the shriek of brakes and tramping footsteps told her that the police had arrived. Nancy ushered Sergeant Malloy and two of his men into the hall, explaining what had happened, and Mrs. Gruen showed them the note she had found.

While the police busied themselves taking foot-prints and fingerprints, Nancy decided to look outside. Taking her pocket flashlight, she went to the porch and peered over the railing.

The beam of her light revealed two slips of paper caught in a barberry bush. Excitedly Nancy examined them. One contained the num-ber 74772. On the other was printed "5 x 7 and one."

Nancy returned to the hall and copied the no-tations, then handed the slips to the police. Sergeant Malloy was inclined to think the long number was the combination of a safe. The other, he admitted, was a puzzle.

"I'll work on them. They're a good clue," he said.

When the police had concluded their investi-gation, the sergeant told Nancy and Hannah he would send a plain-clothes man to watch the house.

"That's good," Mrs. Gruen said. "I don't much care for the job myself."

The following morning Nancy was awakened by the ringing of the telephone. She was delighted when she recognized the deep voice of her father.

"How's everything?" he asked.

When Nancy told him what had happened during the night, Carson Drew expressed concern.

"My plane will get in this afternoon," he said. "In the meantime, I advise you not to go out of the house alone. And look after Hannah. That experience must have been a severe shock to her."

Nancy promised to do as he suggested, and as soon as she had dressed, insisted upon preparing breakfast alone.

"Now don't go pampering me," the housekeeper said.

But she let Nancy cook the cereal and set the table, and she limped slightly instead of bustling around the kitchen as she usually did. After breakfast Nancy announced that Hannah was to take it easy.

"Dad gave special instructions for me to look after you, and I promised him I would. So out you go!" Nancy laughed.

Hannah protested at first, but at last gratefully

withdrew with the morning paper. Nancy tidied the dining room and kitchen. She was just putting away the last plate when Bess Marvin popped her head into the doorway.

"I can't believe my eyes! You in that apron—and Hannah sitting on the porch reading at nine o'clock in the morning!"

Nancy grinned. "Did she tell you about the excitement last night?"

"Yes," Bess said. "And you know what I think? You ought to have a bodyguard."

"Oh, not that!" Nancy replied in amusement. "And thanks for the burglar alarm idea. It did scare someone away."

Bess's plump face dimpled. "I'm glad, and say, I can think of a bodyguard you'd like. There's a certain young man named Ned Nickerson. He's very athletic, I understand—plays quarterback at Emerson College."

"If I needed a bodyguard, he'd do nicely," agreed Nancy, laughing. "But as it happens, I'm very well protected."

Leading her friend to a window, Nancy pointed out a slender man in a gray suit and a slouch hat walking near the driveway entrance.

"One of the plain-clothes men the police sent. It makes me feel very important."

Bess giggled. "As if you were an heiress with a diamond necklace in your bureau drawer?"

"It's a black key, instead," Nancy countered. "And only half of one, at that."

"When's your dad coming home?" Bess asked. When she heard that he would arrive that afternoon, she added, "That's good news. You should celebrate. I'll help you get dinner. I'll make a pie."

Shortly before noon Bess was in the kitchen beating up the meringue for a mountainous lemon pie. Nancy was sitting on a stool beside her, but she was not watching the pie making. She was studying the mysterious numbers she had found in the shrubbery the night before.

The "5 x 7 and one" completely stymied her. It suggested nothing at all. The 74772 was easier. The 7, she thought, might be a River Heights telephone exchange. Whose number could 4772 be?

Suddenly she had an idea. With an excited gasp, she jumped off the stool and rushed into the hall. Quickly she thumbed through the River Heights telephone directory to the W's.

Her hunch was correct. River Heights 7–4772 was listed as the Wangells' number! Rushing back to the kitchen, she told Bess.

"How on earth did you figure that out?" the plump girl gasped.

Nancy said she had wondered ever since she had heard about the diary how Mrs. Wangell had happened to pick Terry to translate it. The whole thing was clear now.

"There's some connection between the Wangells and at least one of Terry's enemies," Nancy explained.

"The one who came here last night and dropped the pieces of paper," Bess exclaimed. "Oh, Nancy, this is awful!"

"I must warn Terry," Nancy said. "I hope he's at the Parkview."

Her heart was pounding excitedly as she telephoned the hotel.

CHAPTER XI

A Lesson in Sleuthing

"I was just going to call you, Nancy," Terry exclaimed. "I worked all morning on Mrs. Wangell's diary, and . . ."

"Then she let you borrow it?"

"No, but I took some pictures with your camera. The black keys we found in Mexico are mentioned in it!"

Nancy was so surprised at Terry's news that she forgot to mention her own discovery.

"I want to see the pictures," she cried. "Bess and I are having lunch here in half an hour. Will you join us?"

Terry thought this a splendid idea. Nancy asked him to try covering his tracks so his enemies would not know where he was going. Half an hour later he arrived riding in a storage company van which had been unloading furniture at the hotel.

"How was that?" He grinned boyishly, setting a brief case on the hall table.

Luncheon was a merry affair, but directly afterward Nancy talked to him seriously about the scraps of paper she had found. Terry could make nothing of the "5 x 7 and one" notation.

"So your would-be burglar had the Wangells' number." The young professor whistled. "I can't stop going there now," he continued. "I'm just beginning to get some valuable facts from the diary. Wait until you see what I brought."

He opened his brief case and laid several photographs of drawings and carbon copies of notes on the table.

"At your suggestion, Nancy," he said, "I left the original notes with the diary. Mrs. Wangell doesn't know I have these."

"Good."

Terry said many of the drawings were a puzzle to him. "To me they seem meaningless, and the diary doesn't say a thing to explain them."

Nancy picked up several of the pictures and studied them. At first she appeared mystified, but suddenly Bess noticed a familiar look on Nancy's face.

"You've figured it out?" she asked excitedly.

"No, but I have an idea."

"That means," said Bess, turning to Terry, "that your puzzle is as good as solved."

"Will you leave these pictures with me for a

while?" Nancy asked. "Perhaps I can find the answer."

"I'd certainly like to have you try," Terry replied. "But here's one I did figure out," he said, handing it over.

The photograph was of page seventy-six in the diary. The upper half of the sheet was covered by handwriting. On the lower part was the rough drawing of a key.

"This page," Terry explained, "was badly torn. The ink used in the drawing had faded out almost entirely."

"It's clear now," Bess remarked.

Terry explained that the lens of a camera can often see more clearly than the human eye.

"That's what happened here."

Nancy already was excitedly reading the strange text.

> "In this sodden wilderness I met a curi-
> ous character, a Swamp Indian. He
> told me of the hiding place of Treasure,
> and of three Black Keys that would un-
> lock the Secret of the Ages."

The girl detective could not make out the next sentence. It seemed to be in a foreign language. When she asked Terry about it, he said it was an Indian dialect. When translated, it meant:

"If Fortune be kind, the Sun and Raindrop keys will help me find this secret myself."

"Then you weren't the only one looking for the secret!" Bess exclaimed, her eyes wide with astonishment.

Underneath the text was the faded outline of a key. Examining it carefully, Nancy could see a design on the stem. One of the symbols in the design looked like the sun. The other could symbolize rain.

"I'll get your half-key, Terry, and we'll compare them," Nancy cried.

Racing upstairs, she secured the key and placed it beside the one in the photograph. The lower half of the key in the picture was identical with the relic Terry had brought from Mexico!

"Are there any other references to the black keys?" Nancy asked excitedly.

Terry nodded and picked up a page of notes he said came from pages ninety and one hundred.

"Here is something I translated from the Spanish. It says, 'Today I heard another story about the Keys of Sun and Raindrop. Whoever finds the secret may be Ruler of Mankind,' and listen to this! '*Look for the Frog.*'"

"It's the same Frog Treasure mentioned on the Mystery Stone!" Nancy exclaimed.

"It looks that way," Terry agreed.

Bess was rereading the text above the key drawing. "Where is the 'sodden wilderness'? And who is the 'Swamp Indian'?" she asked.

Terry said he wished he knew. If it were true that a sea captain owned the diary, even though he was not Mrs. Wangell's grandfather, there was no way to prove it. If there ever had been a name in the book, someone had torn it out, along with several other pages.

"I suspect Mrs. Wangell did the tearing," Bess decided. "She probably didn't want to be caught not telling the truth about her grandfather."

Terry said the rest of the notes he had made that day were interesting, but he doubted that they had any bearing on the mystery of the black keys.

"As a matter of fact, most of the stories are about buried treasure," he remarked. "They're good reading."

"And useful to people like the Wangells and their friends," Nancy declared. "Terry, I was going to ask you not to go back to the Wangells', but I've changed my mind. You do have to go on with what you are doing. Only now, translating and deciphering the diary is just part of the job."

"What do you mean?"

"I mean you're to become a detective."

"A—what?"

Nancy bobbed her head seriously. "The Wangells are dishonest. That's been proved.

They need you for translating the diary. But once you've given them what they want, you won't be safe."

Terry stared, unbelieving. Nancy went on to say that it was necessary to find out more about what they were up to, before the work on the diary was finished.

"It isn't hard to do some simple sleuthing," she said encouragingly. "You see, it's not just the big things—like the diary—that are important. If you want to solve your mystery, you should start noticing the little things, too."

Bess, with a twinkle in her eye, said, "Professor Drew, I think we should have a rehearsal. Pupil Terry Scott will now pretend to be at the Wangell home, detecting."

"And you are Mrs. Wangell, Bess, and I'm Mr. Wangell," Nancy agreed, getting into the spirit of the game. "Now I'll examine you, Terry, on how observing you are. Did you notice the mail in the hall as you came in?"

"Good grief, no! Am I supposed to?"

"Of course. Postmarks and return addresses are important clues. How about the pad on the telephone desk? Any messages?"

"That's snooping."

"I'm afraid a good detective has to snoop," Nancy said. "Now how did Mrs. Wangell— Bess, that is—act during luncheon? Was she nervous?"

"No," Terry Scott decided. "Just hungry."

"That's not exact enough," Nancy told him severely. "She ate two helpings of creamed chicken, four pickles, and a three-inch wedge of cake."

Bess protested. "Nancy, you're mean!"

"I'm just teaching Terry a lesson," Nancy replied, but her eyes showed that she was teasing.

"Well, if that's what detective work is like," Terry said, shaking his head, "I'd better stick to teaching."

Then, apparently, the young professor remembered something. His eyes widened, and he leaned forward excitedly.

"Maybe I do notice things after all," he said.

"What?" both girls asked at once.

"This morning at the Wangells'," Terry said, "while I was in the study, Mrs. Wangell made a telephone call. I just happened to overhear part of it."

"Whom was she calling?" Nancy asked.

"I don't know. But she said, 'I won't forget. The name's King.' She laughed with sort of a sneer, and added, 'Some king he is!' Then she hung up."

CHAPTER XII

Terry Disappears

"YOU *are* a detective, Terry!" Nancy praised the young professor. "The 'King' Mrs. Wangell mentioned must be Conway King—the name Juarez Tino uses."

Terry smiled. "That seems to prove they're in league."

"Keep your eyes open and make sure of that," Nancy begged him. "Try to find out how the Wangells got that diary."

Later that afternoon, when Terry and Bess had gone, Nancy looked at the photographs of the drawings. But she was interrupted by the arrival of her father.

"Oh, it's so good to have you back," Nancy exclaimed, giving him a hug. "Bess has been helping me keep house. You should see the pie she made to celebrate your home-coming."

Carson Drew sighed. "In that case I'll have to stay home and not leave until tomorrow."

"Leave?" Nancy cried. "But, Dad, I have so much to tell you about Terry's mystery. I saw Dr. Anderson, and I think we've found another clue in an old diary."

She accompanied the lawyer to the living-room sofa, and then proceeded to pour out the whole story.

"Well, you have been busy," her father said. "Good results, too. I guess there's no reason now why you shouldn't work on Terry's case. And I have news of my own," he said.

He explained that it had to do with Dr. Pitt. Upon returning to his office, Mr. Drew had found a letter from a man in Baltimore who claimed to be a cousin of the missing professor and demanded a share in any money he might have left.

"Dad!" Nancy exclaimed. "How did he know you're Dr. Pitt's lawyer?"

Mr. Drew said this was exactly what he intended to find out. Since he had to go to Baltimore anyway, in connection with another case, he would look up Pitt's cousin.

Telling Nancy that the person's name was Caswell P. Breed, Mr. Drew handed her his letter. She looked at the scrawled handwriting on the envelope. Nancy felt sure that it was a fake, and told her father so.

"Well, real or not," he said, "I'm going to Baltimore." He looked at his daughter squarely.

"I'd like you to go along and help me, and also meet some friends of mine."

"I'd love to. But first, I want to tell Terry about this Breed person. Maybe he knows him, or Dr. Pitt might have mentioned him."

Nancy quickly telephoned Terry. He was amazed to hear about the letter. The young man had never heard of Breed.

As Nancy put down the telephone, a thought struck her. "Dad," she said, "what gave Breed the idea that Dr. Pitt is dead?"

Mr. Drew looked at Nancy admiringly. "That's exactly what I mean to find out, and quickly," he said.

The lawyer wired ahead for hotel reservations. After supper he and Nancy boarded the evening plane for Baltimore. On the way, Nancy told her father that plain-clothes men were watching the house.

"Just the same I brought the mysterious pictures with me, and the half-key. Terry didn't want me to leave them."

At nine thirty next morning, Nancy and her father taxied through several streets lined with rows of brick houses each with its own white marble steps. Finally they came to the outskirts of the city. The driver stopped in front of a ramshackle dwelling situated next to a factory. C. P. Breed was inscribed on a card nailed above the knocker.

The door was opened by an old man. Mr. Drew introduced himself and Nancy, saying he was the lawyer from River Heights and would like to hear more about Mr. Breed's claim.

The man stroked his whiskered chin and limped inside. "I'll talk to y'all," he said in a high-pitched voice, "but I won't give up the claim. Doc said not to."

Nancy glanced at her father. "When did you last see your cousin?" she asked Mr. Breed.

The old man scratched his head. "He ain't no cousin o' mine. He's my doc, an' a good one, sure enough. Fixed my broken leg what I got at the factory. An' he told me not to give up my claim to any of you lawyers."

"There must be some mistake," Mr. Drew said. He took the letter from his pocket and handed it to the old man. "Did you write this?"

Mr. Breed pulled a pair of spectacles from his vest pocket, adjusted them on his nose, and peered at the letter.

"This is me an' it ain't me," he said. "Breed's my name, but I don't know Dr. Pitt an' I ain't his cousin, an' I didn't write this."

"Do you know who could have sent it?" Nancy asked.

The man said he had not the slightest idea, adding testily, "But I'd like to get hold o' the person who used my name. I'd horsewhip him!" Then he limped to the door with his callers.

On a hunch Nancy asked him if he knew any people named Scott, Graham, Anderson, Tino, King, Porterly, and Wangell. The answer was no in each case.

"You didn't leave out one," the lawyer teased his daughter as they rode off. "But I know what's in your mind; that one of them wanted to work some scheme while we were away, and sent that letter to get us out of town. Which one do you suspect?"

"Juarez Tino," Nancy replied quickly. "I'm sure he's the ringleader of that group. I'm going to phone River Heights and find out if anything's happened."

For the next three hours Mr. Drew worked at the courthouse, while Nancy kept busy at the hotel. First she telephoned Hannah Gruen to be sure everything was all right at home.

"Yes," the housekeeper replied. "Now stop worrying, honey."

"Be extra careful," Nancy warned the woman, and told about the fake letter.

Nancy next turned her attention to the photographs Terry had made of the diary pages. There were nine of them, and at first not one of the drawings suggested a picture. They seemed more like the senseless scrawls of an insane artist.

Then Nancy had an idea. She bought a pad of thin tracing paper, and cut nine sheets to the

exact dimensions of the photographs. On each sheet she made a careful tracing of one of the drawings, using black India ink.

Laying aside the original photographs, Nancy began to juggle the sheets around. She studied them side by side. She placed one sheet over another so that the inked outline underneath showed through the transparent upper sheet.

She shuffled and rearranged them. And very soon she began to make discoveries.

The meaningless lines on three of the drawings, placed one beneath another, suddenly became a picture. Nancy could see a tangle of trees, a large pool of water, and a winding path.

It was the picture, Nancy thought, of some remote tropical wilderness!

Excitedly she took a sheet of tracing paper and joined the outlines of the separate drawings to make a complete picture. Then she searched for other clues.

One of the trees seemed lopsided. It was fan-shaped, like a traveler's palm. But the palm had been neatly split in half!

Was that half-tree a clue? Excitedly, Nancy searched through the rest of the drawings. At last she found what she was looking for—the other half of the fan-shaped tree.

Edging the two sheets together to complete the tree, she made another discovery. The sheets thus placed together completed another picture.

And among the trees and branches was the distinct outline of three keys!

At another spot, where the sheets joined, Nancy found symbols representing the sun, a prostrate man, and a frog. The same figures on the note Terry had found in the tent in Mexico!

"The person who wrote this diary probably had learned in some manner all the directions to the Frog Treasure," Nancy thought wildly. "He didn't dare draw just one picture for fear somebody else would find out the secret!"

Feverishly she worked to decipher the whole picture message. Two other drawings, viewed separately, were nothing but irregular oval blobs. When the drawings were placed one beneath the other, however, the blobs suddenly appeared in pairs.

They were footprints!

Six pair were leading—where? At first Nancy could not answer this riddle. They seemed to lead toward an empty circle.

With painstaking care, she traced the footprints on another sheet of transparent paper. Then she laid them over the drawing of the tropical wilderness.

The result was just what she had suspected it would be. The circle, now, was no longer empty. The footprints led to the rim of the large pool!

Then she placed the sheet over the second

drawing, which revealed the keys and the symbols of frog, prostrate man, and sun.

This time the footprints led to the symbol of the frog!

Nancy could hardly wait for her father to finish his work in Baltimore. She wanted to get home and talk to Terry Scott and show him her discoveries.

But that evening Nancy and her father dined with his friends. The next day there was more work at the courthouse, where Nancy helped the lawyer copy material from old records. At last the work was finished.

The Drews took an early plane for River Heights the following morning. Upon reaching home, Nancy immediately telephoned Terry at his hotel.

"Mr. Scott hasn't been in for two days," the hotel clerk informed her.

"Did he check out?" Nancy asked in amazement.

"No, miss. He just hasn't been around."

Worried, Nancy asked Hannah if she had heard from Terry. Learning that she had not, Nancy wondered if he had changed his mind about staying with the Wangells.

She dialed their number, River Heights 7–4772. Anxiously, she waited. One minute, two minutes, three minutes. There was no answer.

Alarm for Terry's safety now made Nancy's heart beat faster. She telephoned George.

"I'm picking you up in five minutes," she told her startled friend. "I need your help on a research expedition."

Quickly returning the obsidian key to her dressing-table drawer, and putting the photographs in her desk, Nancy caught up her shoulder bag, hurried to the garage and into her car. Within five minutes she reached George Fayne's house. George was waiting at the curb.

"What's on your mind, partner?" she asked.

"Worry," Nancy replied, and told about the disappearance of Terry Scott. "We're going to the Wangells'."

"Ugh!" George commented. "I see trouble ahead."

The Wangell home was built of stone, with gray lions flanking the entrance. Every front window was tightly shuttered, and the porch was bare of furniture.

"Looks as if nobody's at home," George remarked.

"We'll soon see."

After Nancy rang the doorbell, they could hear creaking footsteps inside. But the footsteps hesitated and the person waited until Nancy rang again. Then the door flew open.

A red-faced woman with bleary eyes, her hair tightly clamped in bobby pins, stared out at them. If this was Mrs. Wangell, she looked very different from a newspaper picture of her the girls had once seen.

"What do you want?" she asked suspiciously.

"We're looking for a friend," Nancy stated. "Terence Scott."

"Scott?" said the woman shortly. "Must be another house," and she slammed the door. They heard a bolt slipping into place.

George grinned. "Seems as if we're not wanted."

"Wanted or not, I'm staying here until I do some investigating," Nancy decided. "Did you see those suitcases in the front hall?"

George nodded. "Maybe the Wangells are leaving town."

"If they are, it's for no good reason. George, I saw Officer Riley two blocks south at the intersection. Would you mind bringing him here?"

While George hurried away on her errand, Nancy circled the house. All the side and rear windows were closely shuttered, with the exception of a small, high one in the kitchen. When she looked up at it, Nancy saw a curtain move, as if somebody were watching her.

Then suddenly her attention was directed to the third floor. Fluttering from an attic ventilator, at the rear of the house, was what looked like a man's white handkerchief!

Was it a signal of distress?

CHAPTER XIII

Nancy's Search

WHILE Nancy was still staring upward, she heard a car stop in front of the house. Running around to the front porch, she saw a man and a woman, suitcases in hand, just climbing into a taxicab. The Wangells were leaving!

Before Nancy could reach them, they had slammed the rear door. The man leaned toward the driver with an order, and he started off.

"Wait! Stop!" cried Nancy, racing across the lawn.

Either the driver did not hear her, or he did not want to hear. The cab gathered speed and disappeared around the corner.

Nancy dashed to her own car. They would not get away as easily as that!

But when she turned the corner, the taxi was not in sight. She drove on for several blocks, looking up and down the intersecting streets, but in vain.

"I'll try the railroad station," Nancy thought, and hurried to it. Again no luck.

Her next stop was at the bus station. The Wangells were not there, and waiting passengers said no taxi had stopped at the place for over fifteen minutes.

"Maybe they went to the airport," Nancy guessed. But a telephone call to the information desk gained her no information about the Wangells.

As a last resort she figured they must have engaged the taxi to take them out of town. The young detective hurried to the office of the Winfield Taxi Company. Perhaps the office could communicate with the driver by short wave.

The girl at the desk looked up sullenly as Nancy dashed in. "You can't be in that much of a hurry," she remarked sarcastically.

"But I am," Nancy cried. "One of your drivers had a call to 619 Fairview Avenue. Has he returned?"

"No."

"Then please talk to him over your short-wave radio," said Nancy. "I must find out where his two passengers are going."

"And why should I ask Johnson that?" the girl inquired.

"Because it's very important. It may save a man's life." Briefly, she told her suspicions.

The girl put one hand on her unkempt,

bleached hair, and yawned. "Say, who do you think you are? An FBI agent?"

Nancy saw it was useless to waste any more time arguing. It would be better to get back to Fairview Avenue. George would be there with the policeman.

When she returned to the Wangell house, Nancy saw that George had arrived with Officer Riley. They were just turning the corner of the house. George was talking excitedly.

When she saw Nancy, she gave a sigh of relief. "Hypers, Nancy, I've just about had heart failure. I thought maybe you'd been kidnaped."

"Have you tried to get into the house?" Nancy asked.

Riley nodded. "Rang the doorbell, but no response. The place is locked up tight."

Nancy told them about seeing the couple leave the house, and that she was sure they were the Wangells.

"Did you notice the handkerchief?" she asked.

"What handkerchief?" Riley said.

"I'll show you."

She led the way to the rear of the house. The wisp of white cloth was no longer in sight!

"It was there. I saw it. Out of that attic ventilator," Nancy exclaimed, pointing excitedly.

Officer Riley frowned. "Well, what happened to it?"

"Perhaps it blew away. Or—" Nancy looked grave. "I suspect someone is imprisoned in that house. I'm going to call and see if he answers."

Nancy cupped her hands to her mouth, raised her head, and made a yodeling sound. Then she called, as loudly as she could:

"Terry! Terry Scott! It's Nancy. Can you hear me?"

The three held their breaths, but not a whisper came from the shuttered house.

"Let me try," said George. She in turn called Terry, but there was no reply.

Riley smiled tolerantly. "You sure you haven't been imagining things, Miss Drew?"

Nancy was indignant. "Of course not. I saw a white handkerchief fluttering from that ventilator!" Once more she shouted "Terry!" in a voice as loud as she could muster.

There was no answer from the Wangell house. But next door, a window was flung open and a double-chinned woman leaned out.

"What is it?" she cried. "Is there a fire? Has something happened?"

From the house on the other side an old man, with spectacles resting across his forehead, came bustling out.

"Say, what are you trying to do? Raise the dead?" he asked crossly.

"We hope nobody's dead," commented the

policeman. "These young ladies think someone they know is imprisoned in the house. Have you seen the Wangells lately?"

The old man snorted. "Them? I don't pay them any mind. Never have. Never will. Don't like 'em. Phonies."

"What do you mean?" asked George.

"Just what I say. Phonies. Not decent folks. Not neighborly. Not nice."

"But haven't you noticed anything?" Nancy persisted. "Your house is pretty close to the Wangells. Are you sure you haven't heard any disturbance?"

The old man suddenly straightened. "Yesterday. I'd clean forgot," he said. "I thought it was my radio. I like to keep my radio on. It's down in the library. I don't like this newfangled music and singing. Just classical music."

"Go on, mister," the policeman prodded him.

"I was upstairs yesterday morning, taking my pills. And I heard somebody calling, 'Help, help!' Feeble and far away, you know. I thought, I've got interference. One of those stations cutting in and spoiling my music. That's what I thought."

"Didn't you investigate?" Nancy asked.

"No, young lady. I just went downstairs and fiddled with my radio a bit and I didn't hear anything else."

"Oh, it was Terry. I know it was," cried

Nancy. "Officer, we must go in the house."

The policeman still seemed doubtful. He was about to ask a question, when George gasped, "Look!" and pointed upward.

From the attic ventilator the white handkerchief was once more flying its signal of distress. Riley, as well as the old man, stared wide-eyed.

"Have you a telephone?" the officer asked the neighbor.

The old man nodded and led the way to his back door. When the policeman reappeared, he told Nancy and George that he had called headquarters for reinforcements.

The stout woman who had screamed from the upstairs window now appeared on the scene. She was carrying an ax. Riley grasped the heavy tool and nodded his thanks.

"This will come in handy," he said.

He strode toward a sloping door which led to the outside cellar steps. Testing the door, he found it had been firmly barred from the inside.

"Stand aside, everybody!" he ordered.

He took a mighty swing with the ax, and the heavy door shivered and splintered. Something on the other side fell away with a clatter. Then Riley pried one side of the door open and swung it wide.

"Stay outside, all of you. There may be trouble," he commanded.

The man descended the stone steps. Nancy

and George could see the beam of his flashlight playing into the dark corners of the cellar. A moment later they heard the warning siren of an approaching police car.

Nancy turned to her friend. "George, I'm going inside with the police."

"I'm with you," George declared.

They ran to the front of the house in time to see the police car stop at the curb. Four officers climbed out hastily. Two of them dashed to the rear of the house. The girls met the other two at the front porch.

One of them was Sergeant Malloy, who grinned at Nancy. "You still on the job? It looks as though we will have to make you a special deputy."

Officer Riley appeared at the front door and let them in. Nancy found the dim stairway and hurried upward, with George and two of the police following.

"Terry! Terry, are you all right?" Nancy called.

She expected an answer, but it did not come. The second floor was in complete darkness.

Nancy felt along the wall for a light switch. At last her fingers touched a button. She pressed it, and light flooded a narrow hall.

"Terry!" she called again in alarm.

This time she heard something; not a voice, but

a soft, distinct tapping sound. It was an answering signal and it came from the attic!

Frantically, Nancy, George, and the policemen began opening doors, but each one led to a closet or bedroom. Presently Nancy tried one which she found locked.

"This must be the attic door," she called excitedly. "And Terry Scott's up there. I know he is. Oh, hurry and open the door, officers. Please!"

Sergeant Malloy and Officer Riley braced their shoulders against it. "One! Two! Together now!"

Several swift crashes of their bodies against the door broke the lock. With a splintering sound the door gave way.

CHAPTER XIV

A Grim Story

NANCY was the first one up the narrow stairway to the attic. At her heels came Sergeant Malloy, his flashlight beaming the way ahead.

The Wangell attic seemed to consist of a single storage room, low-roofed and windowless. Nancy looked in vain for the ventilator she had seen from the yard.

But among the shadows she did notice a low door, the key still in the lock. While the police searched behind trunks and dust-covered chests, Nancy went toward the door.

As she did, there came a tap on it. Quickly she opened the door. A figure stumbled toward her.

Terry Scott!

"Terry! Are you hurt?" Nancy gasped.

Though he shook his head, his face was deathly pale and his eyes looked dull and sunken. He tried to smile. One hand wandered feebly to his throat.

"You're ill!" Nancy cried.

The policemen carried him to a chair. Sergeant Malloy reached into a pocket, and brought out a tiny glass vial. Nipping off the end with his thumbnail, he held the vial under Terry's nostrils, and ordered him to take a deep breath.

Almost instantly the color flooded back into Terry's face. His eyes brightened. He moved one hand to his throat.

"Lost my voice yelling," he whispered. "Thanks. You saved my life."

"Let's get him out of here," Sergeant Malloy ordered. "It looks as if he needs medical attention."

"I'll take him to my house," Nancy offered quickly, as they assisted Terry downstairs.

"All right. Then I'll stick around here for a while," Malloy said. "Riley, you go back to your post." Turning to Terry, he added, "I'll get your full story later. Anything special you can tell us now?"

"Look for an old diary with several pages missing," the young scientist managed to say.

Nancy and George drove Terry to the Drew home. Hannah Gruen showed her concern when she saw Professor Scott. After learning that he had been without food for three days, she announced firmly:

"You leave him to me. I know just what he needs."

Hannah insisted that Terry lie down on the living-room sofa. She put some chicken broth on the stove and made toast.

"How can I ever repay you, Nancy?" the young professor murmured over and over after George had gone home.

"By resting and getting your voice back, so you can tell me what happened." Nancy smiled.

When Hannah returned, Nancy announced that she had an errand downtown but would be back as soon as she could. Meanwhile, Terry was to enjoy Mrs. Gruen's cooking and try to sleep.

Nancy hurried out to her car and drove once more to the office of the Winfield Taxi Company. The blond girl at the desk was no longer sullen and flip. She said to Nancy:

"Johnson just phoned in. He's at some farm-house a couple of miles this side of Kirkland."

The driver had told her his two passengers from Fairview Avenue had forbidden him at gun point to turn on the car radio. They had ordered him to drive to Kirkland, where they said they had important business.

Then, as they reached a lonely stretch of wood-land, three miles or so before coming to Kirkland, Wangell had forced Johnson to stop, get out, and walk in the opposite direction.

"We're going to use your cab for a while, Buddy," Wangell had said threateningly. "If

you want it back, you'll find it parked in Kirkland."

Nancy asked the girl if the driver had notified
the police. She did not think so.

"Johnson just called the office a minute ago."

Nancy leaned over the desk, picked up the telephone, and dialed the Wangells' number. Sergeant Malloy answered. Nancy reported what
she had just heard.

"I'll relay that to the force over in Kirkland,"
he said. "I'll tell them to scour the town for the
cab, and the Wangells, too."

"Have you found out anything about them at
the house?" Nancy asked.

"Nary a thing. Not a sign of that diary the
professor mentioned, either. By the way, the
Wangells don't own this house. They only rent
it furnished."

Nancy was disappointed. "Well, I'll appre-
ciate your letting me know if anything turns up."

She was glad to learn, when she returned home,
that Mrs. Gruen's ministrations had worked won-
ders with Terry. He looked like himself again.

Nancy pulled up a hassock and sat down close
beside him. "Don't overtax your voice," she
cautioned, "but please tell me in a few words
what happened at the Wangells'."

"They must have suspected what I was doing
and planned to imprison me until they could get
away," he replied.

"How?"

"You know there were several pages missing from the diary. Mrs. Wangell hinted that they might be in the attic with some other old papers. So I went with her to look."

"And Mr. Wangell sneaked up after you and locked you in?" Nancy asked.

Terry nodded grimly. "Yes, but before he locked the door we had a scuffle. His wife tried to stop us. As I pushed her away, Wangell hit me over the head with a book end. I don't know how long I was knocked out, but when I started coming to, my brain seemed very foggy."

"Drugged," Nancy guessed.

"I think so," Terry answered. "Wangell was standing over me, laughing. It was an awful feeling. He kept asking me questions about the cipher stone. I knew I mustn't give him any information, so I concentrated on you!"

"Me!" Nancy said, amazed.

"Yes." Terry smiled wanly. "I kept saying 'Be a smart detective. Tell them nothing!' You'd be surprised how it seemed to help me."

Terry went on to say that he had found out a few things about the Wangells, however, before his capture.

"They hate each other, for one thing. I'm sure of that. Listening to them talk was like waiting for an explosion. There was an awful tension between the two, even when they weren't quarreling. 'Mrs. Wangell seemed to be afraid of her husband."

"Why?"

"That I didn't learn, but every time she started to find fault with him, he would stop her with a stunt that would send her into a panic. I'll show you."

Terry walked over to the Drews' piano. Clenching his right hand into a fist, he ran his knuckles along the keyboard, hitting the black keys in a loud, quick glissando.

"How strange!" Nancy murmured.

"After Mr. Wangell did that, he'd laugh uproariously," Terry explained. "It had the strangest effect on Mrs. Wangell. She'd clap her hands to her ears and scream, 'No. Earl, no!' as if she were in pain."

"Go on," Nancy urged.

"Here's something a bit more definite," Terry continued. "I think maybe Mrs. Wangell and Mrs. Porterly are sisters."

Nancy was excited. She praised Terry's detecting and asked, "How did you find out?"

"I listened, the way you suggested. Mr. and Mrs. Wangell talked a lot about Miami and a couple down there named Will and Irene. I deduced that Will was short for Wilfred Porterly."

"And his wife?"

"That was easy. Once when the Wangells were arguing, I heard her say, 'You should have listened to Irene and me. We Webster girls at least have common sense.' "

Terry said he had remembered George saying that Mrs. Wangell was Lillian Webster.

"Oh, Terry, this is wonderful!" Nancy cried.

"Glad you think so," he replied, grinning.

"I wonder if the Wangells are on their way now to join the Porterlys in Miami," Nancy mused.

She informed Terry of the Wangells' treatment of the taxi driver, and also told him that the police had searched the house but failed to turn up the diary or any other clues.

Suddenly Terry remembered Nancy's trip to Baltimore, and asked what she had learned there.

"That was just a trick to get us out of town," Nancy answered. "I came back a little too soon for the Wangells. Or did I?" She smiled ruefully. "They got away."

"But you saved me," Terry whispered—his voice was giving out again. "You saw my handker—" The rest was lost.

Nancy insisted he rest again, promising a big surprise at dinnertime that evening. Terry Scott slept for three hours, awakening just as Mr. Drew walked in. The lawyer was deeply concerned when he learned what had happened.

"I had no idea your enemies and Dr. Pitt's would go to such lengths," he said to Terry. "It's amazing what evil men will resort to in trying to acquire a fortune."

This reminded Nancy of her promise. She brought out the photographs of the diary pages and the tracings she had made from them. Terry was intrigued by the footprints leading to the traveler's palm; the symbols of frog, prostrate man, and sun; and the three black keys.

"Amazing!" he murmured, and added in frank admiration, "How do you do it?"

After studying the complete drawing which Nancy had made, the scientist shook his head. "I've never seen a spot that looks like this one," he said. "Too bad it has no directions or points of the compass on it. If I could only locate the cipher stone—"

"Would this help you?" Nancy asked.

She brought out her copy of the slip of paper she had found in the shrubbery with its mysterious notation "5 x 7 and one." Terry could make no more out of it than he had the first time he had glanced at it.

Mrs. Gruen announced supper and they all went to the table. As soon as the meal was over, Mr. Drew drove Terry to his hotel. He promised to retire at once.

At eight o'clock next morning Terry called Nancy on the telephone. For a moment she feared something had gone wrong, but he soon reassured her.

"I did a lot of thinking last night," he said. "I'm sure my place is in Mexico. The Mexican police haven't sent me any report. Maybe they have given up the search for Dr. Pitt. I must find out."

Terry said he had secured a nine-o'clock plane reservation, and was leaving for the airport at once.

"I hate to say good-by this way," he added. "You've been such a good sport, Nancy. But I hope next time I see you, I'll have good news."

Terry said that if she did not hear from him soon, she would know that he was deep in a Mexican jungle looking for his scientist friend.

"Don't you want to take the half-key with you?" Nancy asked, trying to keep her voice calm, but a sudden fear for his safety seized her.

"No. I might lose it. If I need the key, I'll send for it. Anyway, I feel that I'm not going to solve this whole mystery in Mexico. There will be many things you'll have to clear up if you will. I'm depending on you."

"Terry, are you sure you'll be—"

"Now don't worry," he said, laughing. "Well, I must say good-by now."

After she had put down the telephone, Nancy sat lost in thought. No matter how she looked at it, she did not like Terry's sudden decision to start alone for the jungle. What could he do alone against his enemies?

CHAPTER XV

A Hard Decision

AFTER Mr. Drew had been told of Terry's decision, and had left for his office, Nancy reviewed in her mind the swift-moving events of the past twenty-four hours. What was there she could do to help solve the mystery, now that Terry was returning to the scene of his explorations in Mexico?

"I can still try to find out where the Wangells went," she decided. "That may lead to the Porterlys and then to Juarez Tino, and—"

Her thoughts were interrupted by the ringing of the telephone. The caller was George, and Nancy told her about Terry. Two minutes later it rang again. Sergeant Malloy was reporting failure in locating the Wangells.

"The Kirkland police turned the town inside out. No tips on where those folks went. You got anything else to suggest?"

"Florida."

"What?"

"My guess is," Nancy replied, "that the Wan-gells will join the Porterlys in Florida."

Malloy seemed to be intrigued with the idea that the two wives might be sisters. He said the police would communicate with Florida authorities to try to find the couples in the South.

When Bess Marvin dropped in a few minutes later Nancy was strumming idly on the piano in the living room.

"George phoned me," Bess said excitedly. "Told me all about yesterday. She says Terry's left town, bag and baggage, and didn't say good-by to anyone but you. Oh, dear, I wish I'd been home for the excitement, but I suppose I'd have been scared green."

Nancy smiled, but she made no comment.

"You wouldn't be feeling lonesome for Terry already?" her friend asked slyly. "Or is it the plain-clothes men you miss? I notice they've left."

"They're on duty only at night now," Nancy answered. "But I'm not lonesome. I'm trying to puzzle something out," she declared. "Bess, do you know what five times seven and one are?"

"Why, thirty-six."

"Yes. And I've just been counting, Bess. There are exactly thirty-six black keys on the piano."

She told Bess about Mr. Wangell's trick of

frightening his wife. "Like this." Nancy illustrated by running her knuckles over the keyboard as Terry had done the day before.

"Nancy, are you trying to say there's some connection between that slip of paper you found in the shrubbery and Wangell's trick of scaring his wife?"

"I don't know. But that stunt at the piano must have reminded Mrs. Wangell of something very unpleasant. It may have been some sort of a threat."

"Nancy, you make me positively shudder!"

"Never mind. Here's something quite different and more tuneful."

Nancy played Chopin's Etude on the black keys while Bess listened admiringly.

"I never knew you could play anything as beautiful as that just on the black keys," she said as Nancy finished. "All I can manage on black keys is boom-boom-boom."

Bess was demonstrating her musicianship on the bass notes of the piano, while Nancy dubbed in a treble melody, when George Fayne stalked into the room, a tennis racket in her hand.

"Whatever are you two doing?" she wanted to know. "It sounds like a double nightmare."

Bess giggled, saying that she and Nancy were practicing a duet for a piano recital.

"In the River Heights Kindergarten Band?" George remarked. "I thought you'd be busy

solving the disappearance of the Wicked Wangells."

"That's what started this," Nancy said, and
told the girl about Mr. Wangell's strange per-
formance at the piano.

George grimaced. "I'm changing my opinion
of the Wangells. They're not just the Wicked
Wangells. They're the Wicked, Wacky Wangells.
How about a set of tennis doubles with Doris
Harrison?"

Nancy agreed, but it was apparent during their
drive to the courts to meet Doris that her mind
was not on tennis.

"How would you two like to take a trip to
Florida?" she asked her friends suddenly.

"Love to," George declared. "But my bank
account would never stand the strain."

"Neither would mine after that trip to New
York," Bess sighed. "But wouldn't I just love to
go! Moonlight nights on the beach, the perfume
of orange blossoms—"

"But I doubt if that would interest Nancy,"
George interrupted. "What's on your mind, Detective Drew?"

"Terry Scott, I'll bet," Bess spoke up. "Now
admit it, Nancy. Isn't Terry the attraction in
Florida?"

Nancy ignored the teasing, and explained that
Terry was on his way to Mexico, not Florida.
"If anybody is on my mind, it's the Wangells and

the Porterlys." She told about the possibility of the wives being sisters, and her deduction that the two families might be meeting in Florida.

"My advice is to stay away from there," George said sternly. "I don't want those awful people feeding you to the alligators."

"Oh, don't say such things!" Bess reprimanded her cousin. "You give me the shivers."

By this time the girls had reached the Tennis Club, and Nancy promised to put mystery aside for an hour. Doris had reserved a court and in the twirl of rackets became Bess's partner.

The girls played a good game and seemed to be evenly matched. Each side won a set. As the third set stood five games even, Nancy suddenly found herself wondering if Terry had been followed. Maybe— Racket out of position, she missed the ball.

"Forty all!" George drawled.

Nancy double-faulted and a moment later Bess and Doris won the two needed points.

Nancy chided herself for her temporary lapse, and settled down to some of the best tennis she had ever played. She and George won the deciding set.

"Good fun," Doris declared as the others got into their car, "even though I lost."

As soon as Nancy reached home, she sped to the telephone to call Sergeant Malloy. She must find out the latest developments before asking her father a very important question.

"Nothing new on the Wangells," the officer said. "But we have a report on Wilfred Porterly His driver's license is okay. But according to the records, he hasn't owned a car since 1929, so the car registration was forged and the license plates stolen."

"Did the Miami police find him at his home?" Nancy asked.

"No, but they'll keep an eye out for him. Remember that Tropical Sun Fruit Company Porterly talked about? There's no such business either in Miami or any other place in the State of Florida. Porterly uses that as a blind. Makes him sound respectable."

"What is his business?"

"If it had a name, it would probably be Shady Deals Incorporated. A lot of the deals have been pretty fancy rackets. At one time, for instance, he was connected with some art dealers."

"The Wangells," thought Nancy. "And now the 'fancy racket' is cashing in on an old treasure."

Nancy was more eager than ever to carry on a search in Florida. After lunch she broached the subject to her father.

"Dad, do you suppose you could manage a Florida vacation next week?"

"I'm afraid not," he replied. "I must be in court Wednesday."

"Then how about my taking that field trip with Professor Anderson? It sounds interesting. If he lets me join his students, will you give me money for the trip?"

The lawyer's eyes twinkled. "If I furnish the capital, seems to me I deserve a statement of some kind. Are you really so fascinated by Indian culture—or do you want to keep your eye on Professor Anderson?" he teased.

"All right, Dad. I'll own up. You'd never let me go to Florida alone."

"And?"

"You see, it's not just Dr. Anderson who is heading for Florida. My guess is that Wilfred Porterly is there this minute. And the Wangells are on their way."

"I see," Mr. Drew said. "But what made you think of getting to Florida by trying to join Dr. Anderson's group?"

Nancy said there were several reasons. She believed it was not just his duties as a teacher that were taking Dr. Anderson to Florida. It might well have to do with the mystery of the black keys and the Frog Treasure.

"Maybe we can work together," she said. "Anyway, if I locate the Wangells, I may need a man's help."

"Right you are," the lawyer agreed. "Well, if you will go with the rest of the class, I'll give you the money. But I'm wondering if Dr. Anderson will permit it. You're not a student of his, my dear."

Nancy smiled confidently. "No. But several who are going on the trip are specials. They come from various places." She gave her father a hug. "Thanks a million," she said. "I'll phone for an appointment to talk it over."

When Nancy faced the professor in his office the following Monday morning, she did not feel so confident, however. Dr. Anderson was not very cordial.

"I suppose you know, Miss Drew, that you are a bit late. The students who have registered for the trip have already completed their preparatory work."

"I know it's highly irregular, Dr. Anderson. But I've done some reading about American Indians, ancient and modern. And I was hoping you'd accept me as a sort of special student."

The professor narrowed his eyes. "Isn't it a bit sudden, your interest in this field trip?"

Nancy could not help smiling. "I'll be honest with you, Dr. Anderson. It's not just interest in your subject that prompted my visit. I want to do some research of my own in Florida. And I need you as a sort of—bodyguard."

Perhaps it was Nancy's smile—or her show of honesty—that brought about a change in his manner. The professor did not exactly smile back, but his eyes softened. There was a suggestion of compromise in his voice when he spoke again.

"As you say, it is highly irregular. But I'll tell you what I'll do."

"Yes?" Nancy asked hopefully.

"I'm giving my students here a quiz on the work we've covered so far. If you can pass that quiz, you may accompany us to Florida."

Nancy's pulse quickened. "I'll try it," she said. "Thank you."

CHAPTER XVI

A Smoke Screen

DR. ANDERSON blinked, unbelieving, when Nancy said she would take the quiz.

"When is it?" she asked.

"This afternoon at three," the professor replied.

Nancy looked at her watch. It was ten thirty. She had a few hours to study!

Eager to use her time to advantage, Nancy hurried to the college library. There the librarian pointed out the books used for Dr. Anderson's course in American Indian Culture.

"And this should help you," the woman said, giving Nancy a typewritten sheet. "It's an outline of the work covered each month."

The outline stated that the subjects assigned for the past month were *The Aztecs of Mexico* and *Early Indian Tribes in Florida*.

Fortunately, Nancy had brought a notebook and her fountain pen. She read all the chapters on Florida Indians, and made notes on the facts which seemed most important about the ancient Aztecs.

She hardly took time for lunch, studying her notes while she ate a sandwich in the cafeteria. When she had memorized them, she tried to fit them in with what Terry had told her about Mexico. After lunch she returned to the library and did more reading until it was time to go to class.

As the students flocked in to take their seats, one of the girls looked at Nancy and smiled.

"Hello," she said. "Are you going on our field trip?"

"I hope so. But I have to pass the quiz first."

Her neighbor rolled her eyes. "So do we all! I'll wish you luck if you wish me luck."

"That's fair enough." Nancy laughed.

Professor Anderson arose from behind his desk. Nancy felt his eyes upon her, but he did not smile.

"Please remember that none of you will be given special consideration," he said, looking straight at Nancy. "If you know the subject, you will pass. If you do not know the answers, you will fail."

He gave out the quiz sheets and the blue books. Immediately Nancy began writing down her answers.

Her hours in the library, she discovered, had been well spent. The questions about Florida Indians and their customs were easy. So were those on Cortez, the Spanish conqueror of the Aztecs, and the fabulously wealthy Emperor Montezuma.

Nancy enjoyed answering the question: *Why has Texcoco been called the Athens of America?* She explained that Texcoco was, to ancient Mexico, what Athens had been to Greece—a center of culture and learning. Its pagan chief was a wise man who built temples and gardens. He improved the laws of his people and encouraged the arts.

The fourth question on the quiz surprised Nancy. "What is obsidian? For what was it used?"

How thankful she was that she had listened to Terry's description of the half-key!

"Obsidian," she wrote, "is a glassy volcanic rock. It was used by the ancient Mexicans for making spearheads, arrow points, knives, mirrors, keys, and other objects."

But to the last question she had no answer at all: *Who were the Zapotecs? Where and when did they live?*

She did not remember having read anything about the Zapotecs. Terry Scott had never mentioned them.

She had to leave the question blank!

At the end of the period, Professor Anderson asked the students to put their quiz books on his desk. When Nancy left hers, she hoped he would speak to her. But he only returned her smile with a stern nod.

"He'll be a hard marker," Nancy thought woefully.

After class her friendly neighbor was waiting with two other girls.

"How did you make out?"

Nancy sighed. "I couldn't answer the question about the Zapotecs."

Her friend grinned. "Anderson's a mean old crow for asking that one. He didn't give it in lectures. He just said we could look it up."

One of the other girls said, "How about introducing us, Fran? Just to be polite."

Fran laughed and asked Nancy what her name was. Then she said that she was Frances Oakes, and she introduced her friends as Marilyn Maury and Grace James.

"Are you coming to Florida with us?" Grace asked hopefully.

Nancy said that she planned to go if she passed the quiz.

"That's the big 'if' for all of us," Marilyn said with a sigh.

She told Nancy that she and her friends were tired, and hungry as bears. They were going to her room for something to pep them up. Wouldn't Nancy join them?

"We'll need plenty of stimulation to stand the strain of waiting until tomorrow," Fran groaned.

"What happens tomorrow?" Nancy asked. "Quiz grades will be posted."

She linked arms with Nancy, and they followed the other two girls over to the dormitory, where they made hot cocoa.

"We have that old Mexican priest Montezuma to thank for this." Fran giggled. "He's said to have introduced *cacao* to the world."

"I'm glad that wasn't on the quiz," Nancy replied with a smile. "I never heard it."

While the girls munched cookies, she told them about her decision to take the quiz. She said she hoped, if she could go to Florida, to do some research on her own.

"Oh, I hope you can go," said Fran. "Marilyn and Grace are rooming together at the hotel, but I don't have a roommate. I'd love it if you'd room with me."

"Please do," Grace pleaded. "We'll have such fun, the four of us."

Nancy liked all the girls, especially Fran, and she agreed to share her new friend's room if Professor Anderson would allow her to go with the class.

"What time tomorrow will he post the grades?" she asked.

"He promised they'd go up by five o'clock," Fran answered. "I'll call you as soon as I know them myself."

The night after the quiz was a restless one for

Nancy. She tossed in bed, unable to relax. The quiz questions, and the answers she had given, revolved like a pin wheel in her brain.

Next morning, she decided to look up the answer to the question she had missed. From the encyclopedia, she learned that the Zapotecs were an important tribe of Mexican Indians. They had resisted invasions by the Aztecs and their culture had been one of the highest in that country.

After reading the article, Nancy's hopes sank. That does it, she thought. Her ignorance would seem inexcusable to Professor Anderson. She would flunk the quiz.

"And Dad will never let me go to Florida alone," she sighed.

At luncheon, Carson Drew noticed that Nancy was not eating with her usual appetite. "Is that quiz about the Indians on your mind?" he asked kindly.

Nancy admitted that it was. Then she changed the subject and tried to act cheerful. But after her father had left for his office, she looked at her watch anxiously. How could she spend those four long hours, waiting for Fran to call?

Fate answered that question.

Shortly after one thirty, the River Heights fire siren blasted suddenly, and Mrs. Gruen came hurrying from the kitchen.

"It's our district," the housekeeper announced.

"That fire must be right in this neighborhood."

She and Nancy rushed out to the front porch. Sure enough, black smoke was pouring from the Hackney house, two doors up the street.

Nancy and Hannah raced across the lawns, reaching the scene before the fire engines. From somewhere in the rear of the house, Nancy heard a woman screaming. Leaving Mrs. Gruen, she ran to the back door in time to see Mrs. Hackney come staggering out, carrying her year-old baby. She was crying hysterically.

"I don't know where Johnny is. Where is my boy Johnny?" she wailed. The woman seemed bewildered.

Nancy knew that Johnny was the other Hackney child, a husky three-year-old.

"I'll find him!" she offered.

Before Hannah Gruen could protest, Nancy ran into the smoke-filled house. She stopped in the kitchen long enough to drench a turkish towel with water. Then she went through the house, searching each room.

As yet, no flames were visible, but suffocating billows of smoke eddied around her. The smoke, she noticed, had an oily, pungent odor.

"Johnny, Johnny!" she called. At last she heard an answering whimper.

Groping her way to an upstairs room, she found the boy on the floor, rubbing his eyes and coughing. Nancy caught him up in her arms and let him bury his face in the cool towel. Then, fighting her way through the smoke once more, she stumbled down the stairway and out of doors, just as the firemen arrived.

Mrs. Hackney met Nancy with a welcoming cry. "Oh, my child! My own Johnny!" When she saw the little fellow smile, she stopped sobbing and turned to the rescuer. "Nancy, you saved his life!"

Meanwhile, the firemen had gone inside the house. Presently one of them emerged from the cellar carrying a big galvanized pail from which black smoke billowed.

The fireman came toward Mrs. Hackney. "Good thing you called us," he said, showing her several black, smoldering rags. "Here's your trouble, Mrs. Hackney. Know anything about this?"

Mrs. Hackney stared. "N-no. Where did you find that?"

"The hot-air pipe from your furnace was stuffed with these rags. They've got oil on 'em and some sort of chemical. That's what made the terrible smoke in your house."

"Mercy!" cried Mrs. Hackney. "Whoever would do a crazy thing like that?"

Nancy shuddered. The Drews' front door had been left open. The same firebug might have gone into their house!

Not seeing Hannah to call to, she hurried home

alone. The door was still open, so Nancy knew the housekeeper was not back.

Quickly she went to the kitchen and opened the cellar door. There was no sign of smoke. She was breathing a sigh of relief, when she heard a stifled cough.

Nancy's heart pounded. The man who had started the fire at the Hackneys'—was he upstairs, perhaps starting a fire?

Then another thought came to her. Had he set the Hackney fire to lure her and Hannah away, so he would have time to look for something—and steal it?

Nancy thought with regret of the plain-clothes man who had been on guard during the day. If only he had not been dismissed!

She tiptoed through the kitchen, and cautiously crept through the lower hall and up the carpeted stairway.

As she reached the upper hall, Nancy heard a soft click—the sound of a doorknob turning. Then she saw her bedroom door open and a figure emerge.

The figure turned, saw her, and straightened. It was Juarez Tino! He was clenching something black in his hand.

Terry Scott's half-key!

CHAPTER XVII

A Need for Help

JUAREZ TINO gasped in astonishment. He stood irresolute, then wheeled and started for the back stairs.

"Oh, no, you don't!" Nancy cried. With a lightning lunge she was after him, reaching for his clenched right hand.

"Give me that key!" she demanded.

"I will not!" Juarez muttered.

Nancy was desperate now. She tore at his right hand with both of her own and managed, for a moment, to wrest the key from the man's grasp.

But not for long. With an angry oath, Juarez wrenched his arms free and pushed her violently through the bedroom doorway. Prying her fingers loose, he once more took possession of the key, dropping it into his breast pocket.

"Help! Help!" Nancy screamed, hoping Mrs. Gruen was near the house.

"That won't do you any good," Juarez leered

triumphantly, and forced Nancy to her knees. "I'll teach you," he sneered.

His knee against her back, he sent her sprawling face downward, and bound her ankles with his necktie. Then he seized both her hands and pinned them behind her. With a handkerchief, he tied her wrists together.

Next, Juarez tore a blanket from her bed and stretched it on the floor. Nancy twisted and thrashed away from him. Though she was powerless to escape, the struggle delayed him a few seconds. She tried to scream again, but Juarez clamped a hand over her mouth.

"When I get through with you, you won't be able to talk," the swarthy man threatened.

He whipped a handkerchief out of his breast pocket and gagged her. As he pulled out the handkerchief, Nancy saw the half-key fly through the air, though she did not see it land.

Juarez apparently did not know he had lost it. He rolled her over and over in the blanket, until it encased her from toe to shoulders. Next, he tied it with a sheet.

He dragged her into Mr. Drew's bedroom, and pushed her out of sight under the four-poster bed.

"You should have stayed at the fire a while longer, Detective Drew," he sneered. "I didn't expect you back so soon."

At that moment the front door slammed, and

Hannah Gruen called, "Nancy, are you home?"
When there was no answer, she came up the
front stairway.

With a low oath, Juarez left the room. Creaking footsteps told Nancy he was sneaking down
the back steps.

If only she could scream Hannah's name! She
could barely moan.

The housekeeper heard the moan, however.
Perplexed, she opened the door to Nancy's room.
Nancy heard her exclamation of alarm when she
saw the bed pulled apart, the bureau drawers in
disarray.

Nancy, meanwhile, had managed to roll out
from under her father's big bed. She heaved
against the night table and unbalanced the lamp.
Its crash brought Mrs. Gruen to her side immediately.

"Nancy!"

Hands trembling, she removed the gag from
the girl's mouth. As she untied the sheet, Nancy
explained what had happened.

"Juarez Tino started that fire and trussed you
up?" Hannah Gruen cried. "If I ever get my
hands on that villain—!"

She flew to the window. Not seeing him, she
rushed to the telephone. As Mrs. Gruen dialed
police headquarters, she stormed:

"They shouldn't have let that plain-clothes

man go. Leaving you here at the mercy of that maniac! I'm going to tell those policemen a thing or two!"

Nancy got to her feet stiffly, rubbing her arms to bring back the circulation. Returning to her own room, she stood deep in thought, wondering about the key. It was not in sight. Had Juarez discovered his loss and retrieved the key?

But Nancy did not think he had gone back into her room. Hopeful that he had not taken the precious relic with him, she examined every inch of carpet. The key was not in sight.

Hannah called, "Nancy, I have Sergeant Malloy on the phone. He wants to talk to you."

The officer asked a number of questions about Juarez Tino. He said he would put several of his men on the thief's trail immediately.

"We'll comb this town," he declared, "and every other town within a dozen miles. We'll start at once. I'll be up to see you later."

After Nancy had hung up, Mrs. Gruen joined in the search for the missing obsidian key. When neither of them could find it in Nancy's room, they were forced to admit that Juarez must have taken it with him.

Nancy was blaming herself for not having chosen a safer hiding place, when she heard a car in the driveway. Glancing from the window, she saw Sergeant Malloy step out.

"You found him?" she asked excitedly, after

Hannah admitted the policeman and brought him upstairs.

"Not yet, but the men are out looking. I stopped in to get a full report on what happened, and to tell you we heard from Macon, Georgia."

"About the Wangells?"

"No. The Porterlys. The police there say a couple who gypped a gas station attendant, and rode off just before the police got our message, were probably the Porterlys. The Macon police are trying to track them down."

"I thought they were in Florida already," Nancy said. "I wonder when the Wangells expect to meet them."

The officer said he wished he knew. Malloy made an examination of the premises. He was just leaving when George and Bess came in. When Nancy walked outside with him to conclude her conversation, Mrs. Gruen told them the story.

"Hypers, Nancy!" said George, when she returned. "Talk about a cat having nine lives! This must be your forty-ninth!"

"That awful man!" Bess wailed. "He might have killed you!"

George gave her friend a searching glance. "You don't seem very happy," she remarked. "Aren't you glad to be alive?"

"I'm afraid Juarez took Terry's key with him. Terry will never forgive me!"

George and Bess made Nancy tell everything that had happened, moment by moment. They ended by re-enacting the drama together, with Nancy's bedroom key substituting for the black half-key.

George suddenly had an inspiration. "Which blanket did Juarez use?"

"The dark navy one from my bed. It's in Dad's room on a chair."

George raced into Mr. Drew's bedroom and spread the blanket on the floor. Caught in the fleecy wool was the black half-key! It was hardly noticeable against the navy color.

"George! You found it!" cried Nancy, delirious with joy.

"Uh-huh. Drew and Fayne, detective agency at your service!"

In the midst of the excitement, the telephone rang. Hannah answered, then called up the stairway, "It's for you, Nancy. The girl says her name's Frances Oakes."

Nancy sobered at once. On the way to her father's telephone, she tried to calm herself.

This was a decisive moment. She was about to learn whether she had passed Dr. Anderson's quiz. Upon this call would depend her chance of a trip to Florida to continue her quest of the black keys and the Frog Treasure!

CHAPTER XVIII

Winning a Friend

"HELLO, Fran," Nancy said into the telephone, her heart thumping. "What's the news?"

"Nancy, you made it! I don't see how you did it without going to class. But you passed!"

Nancy had to giggle, she felt so relieved. "I was lucky, I guess. How did you girls make out?"

"We passed, and we're thrilled you're going to Florida with us."

Nancy asked when the trip would start and from what point.

"Dr. Anderson has chartered a plane for to-morrow at midnight. It leaves from the airport near the Institute," Fran replied.

"Wonderful!" Nancy exclaimed. "I'll be there. Any special clothes I should bring?"

"A few cotton dresses, slacks or dungarees, and high-laced boots for trips in swampy terrain. The going will be rough some places, Professor Anderson says.   Snakes and things."

"Mmm!   What else?"

"Bring a bathing suit—naturally.   Say, do you like to water ski?"

"Love to."

"My cousin, Jack Walker, who lives in Miami, has a motorboat," Fran said.   "When we're not working, maybe we can go out with him."

Nancy promised to meet Fran at her dormitory for dinner the next evening.   Then she said good-by, and hurried to tell the good news to Bess, George, and Hannah.

"I don't envy you one bit," exclaimed Bess. "I'm afraid of crocodiles."

"When I was about ten years old," said George reminiscently, "my family took me to Key West. We ate turtle steak and lime pie."

"What kind of pie is that?" asked Mrs. Gruen, interested at once in a new dish.

"It's made with limes grown on the Keys." Suddenly she snapped her fingers.   "Maybe the treasure is buried on one of the Florida Keys!" she exclaimed.

"What treasure?" Bess asked.

"The Frog Treasure.   The ancient secret which Terry thinks is hidden in a jade or silver frog."

"I thought it was in Mexico," Bess said.   "You mean Juarez Tino found out where it's buried?"

"Or buried it there himself after he brought it

from Mexico," George replied. "Remember how
Wangell scared his wife, striking those black keys
on the piano? Maybe it was a sort of pun."

"You mean," Nancy spoke up, "that Wangell
knew the story from Juarez and might have been
reminding Mrs. Wangell of something that happened on a *Black Key* in Florida?"

"Exactly."

"The way it bothered her, it must have been
something awful," Bess declared. "Burying a
treasure isn't so awful."

"That's right," Nancy said, frowning. "There
must have been something more to it than just
that. But anyway, if Juarez Tino had the treasure, why would he still want the half-key?"

"I didn't think of that," said George.

Nancy decided to look at a map of the territory
to which she was going. Perhaps an answer to
the problem would present itself. Hurrying to
the bookcase, she sought a detailed map of the
Florida Keys in an atlas.

As the cousins looked over her shoulder, Nancy
ran her finger along the many Florida islands,
scanning them quickly for their names: Key
Largo, Plantation Key, Tropical Key, Windley
Island, Matecumbe Key.

"No Black Key yet," she sighed.

They continued to examine the map in silence
for several seconds.

"Here it says 'Ten Thousand Islands,' " Bess

remarked. "I wonder if all of them have names."

Mrs. Gruen shook her head in astonishment. "My! I didn't know one state could have so many islands. Why do they call them Keys?"

Nancy said she was glad Hannah had not questioned her on that three days before. In reading about Florida for the quiz, she had learned that the Spanish word for little island was "cayo." English settlers who had come to Florida after the Spanish had thought the word was "key."

"Here's a strange one," Nancy went on. "*Key West* really means 'island of bones.'"

"How horrible!" Bess interrupted. "Should I ask why?"

Nancy smiled. "The first white men to sail there found a lot of Indian bones—there must have been a big tribal battle at one time. They called the place *Cayo Huesto*.

"Which sure sounds like Key West," George said. "I don't blame those early English settlers."

Once more Nancy ran her finger along the fine print on the map. No Black Key listed. But probably many of the small islands had names known only locally, she concluded. As soon as she reached Florida, Nancy would find out if there were an island called Black Key.

It was possible that such an island might be uninhabited and unexplored. A perfect spot for hiding a captive—like Dr. Joshua Pitt!

Long after Bess and George had left, Nancy continued to brood over this possibility. Alternately she was excited about the prospect of finding the elderly professor hidden there, and afraid he might have been starved or tortured by Juarez Tino and his friends.

A voice from the second floor brought her back to reality. "If you don't come and see about your clothes, Nancy, you won't be ready to go."

"Coming, Hannah."

Nancy went upstairs and picked out a few summer dresses, skirts, and sweaters. Then as Hannah started the packing, Nancy went downtown to buy heavy, high-laced boots.

Upon her return Hannah said that Ned Nickerson had telephoned. Hearing of Nancy's plan to join Dr. Anderson's expedition, he had said he would be down next day to drive her to Clifton Institute.

"He's expecting to take you to lunch and spend part of the afternoon with you," the housekeeper reported. "That means you'll have to be ready by one o'clock."

Nancy was pleased that Ned was coming. Next morning, after kissing her father good-by and promising to write often and not take long chances in her sleuthing, she and Hannah went to Nancy's bedroom to finish the packing. As the housekeeper opened the young detective's handkerchief drawer, she found Terry Scott's half-key.

"While you're away, it seems to me you ought to put this in a safer place," she advised.

"You're right," Nancy admitted. "From now on, I'm going to know where it is every minute."

She fastened the half-key securely to a narrow but strong, flesh-colored ribbon some eighteen inches long. Then she tied the ribbon and slipped it over her head, hiding the key inside her blouse.

"I should have thought of this before Juarez came here," she told the housekeeper.

"I hope," said motherly Mrs. Gruen, "that you'll think twice, and run as fast as you can, if you ever see that man again."

"I promise." Nancy laughed.

Bess and George arrived just as Ned drove up, and wished Nancy a wonderful trip to Florida.

"Say, what's in here?" Ned asked as he picked up a suitcase with the heavy boots in it. "Bricks?"

"No, silly," George replied. "A microscope, an atlas, a nice fat encyclopedia—"

Everyone laughed but Bess. There were tears in her eyes. She was so afraid something might happen to Nancy in Florida if those desperate characters found her trying to thwart their plans!

Nancy read the girl's thoughts and gave her an extra kiss. Then she stepped into Ned's car and was off.

During luncheon Ned teasingly declared he believed he would go all the way to the Keys. What fun was it playing football if Nancy was

not in the stands? And afterward a dance date
with some other girl!

The hours sped by quickly. Before they
realized it, the time had come for Ned to leave
Nancy at Fran Oakes's dormitory.

After a leisurely evening with Fran and her
friends, Nancy taxied with them to the airport.
Dr. Anderson was there and most of the students
who were taking the trip.

"Mind if I sit next to the professor on the
plane?" Nancy asked her friends.

"You mean you really want to?" Grace James
gasped.

"Really and truly. We have a few things to
discuss."

Word was passed around, and when the students took seats, Nancy found that the one next
to Dr. Anderson had been left for her. She said,
"Do you mind?" and pretended not to notice
when the professor gave her a cold, unfriendly
stare.

The engine roared, the propellers spun. The
plane sped down the runway and lifted gently
into the midnight sky.

Nancy waited for the professor's face to un-
freeze in a smile. But he stared straight ahead.

"I looked up the answer to the question I
missed on the quiz. About the Zapotecs," she
said. The professor merely nodded.

Then Nancy mentioned the Indian tribes in

Florida. She spoke guardedly of a diary which described the Florida Indians and their legends. It had been written, she said, partially in an Indian tongue.

"Might have been Timucuan," growled Dr. Anderson. "At the time of the conquest, Timucuan was the language known all over Florida."

After he said that, his face flushed and his eyes got fiery.

"Look here, Miss Drew, why don't you admit you've been working for Terry Scott—that you still work for him? Are you meeting him in Florida?"

"No," said Nancy quietly. "Terry has gone to Mexico."

Dr. Anderson exclaimed, "Mexico! What has he found out? Why has he gone back there?"

When Nancy did not immediately reply, he burst out petulantly, "I suppose he took that half-key with him. And it isn't his. He has no right to it!"

CHAPTER XIX

Out of Control!

NANCY winced. Terry had no right to the obsidian key? Who had a right to it if Professor Scott did not?

If Dr. Anderson only knew that the key was not two feet from him, he might feel even more disgruntled and suspicious than he was!

"Terry Scott has no more right to it than Dr. Graham and I have," Professor Anderson continued in an angry tone.

Nancy breathed easier. Smiling, she said, "Perhaps not. But someone has to keep it."

"Well," the professor said testily, "Terry Scott is acting mighty secretive about the whole thing. Why didn't he inform me that he was going to Mexico?"

Nancy tried to keep her voice calm and unruffled. "As you know, Terry is on leave from his classes at Keystone this year. While you and

Dr. Graham are busy with your teaching, he naturally feels that he ought to be trying to solve the ancient mystery."

"He'll make certain that he appropriates the honor and the glory, too," Dr. Anderson complained bitterly.

"I'm sure that's not his intention, professor."

Nancy assured him that Terry's main concern was the disappearance of Joshua Pitt. Both she and Terry were fearful the doctor was being held a prisoner.

Dr. Anderson did not agree. He still had a feeling that the elderly professor was hunting for the treasure by himself.

"Anyway," Nancy went on, "I'm sure that as soon as Terry learns anything definite, he'll tell both you and Dr. Graham."

"That old fuss-budget!" the professor scoffed.

Nancy laughed. "You know what I think, Dr. Anderson? You're all jealous of one another. Talk about Terry being secretive! I'll bet right now you have a secret you're not telling either Terry or Dr. Graham."

Nancy saw a slow flush come to Dr. Anderson's face, and she pressed her advantage.

"For instance, this trip to Florida. You have chosen that spot for the field trip because you think that something—or someone—is hidden there. Haven't you?"

The professor was taken by surprise. He

turned to peer at her, a startled look in his eyes. This young girl was reading his mind!

"For a girl your age, you seem to know a lot of answers." He sighed. "I may as well admit the truth. I suspect the treasure may be buried in Florida, and Dr. Pitt and Juarez know this."

"Why?"

Professor Anderson told her that during Juarez Tino's call on him at Clifton, the man had accidentally dropped a hint. He had mentioned the fact that the ancient Indians of Mexico and Florida had a great deal in common in their state of civilization.

"I'm sure he didn't figure that out himself," Dr. Anderson said. "He got it from Pitt. Right away I suspected he'd been with Pitt in Florida and was double-crossing him."

"Did you accuse him of that?" Nancy asked excitedly.

The professor nodded. "Juarez swore he hadn't been near Florida. But I knew he was lying."

"Wouldn't he tell you anything about Dr. Pitt?"

"He was so furious at me for guessing it, that he raised his price. That was when I threw him out of my office."

"I can't blame you for that," said Nancy. "And it fits right in with a theory of mine." She told about Terry and the Wangells and the trick on the black piano keys. "Only, I'm positive Dr. Pitt and Juarez are enemies, not friends."

She also told him about the warning message at the Drew door, and of her recent encounter with Juarez, when he had bound and gagged her, and shoved her under a bed.

"He'd probably treat a man even worse," she added.

Dr. Anderson's eyes widened. "You're a plucky girl, Miss Drew!" he said. There was a new respect for the young girl in his voice.

He hesitated. Finally his face relaxed in a broad smile.

"I don't mind saying I admire your spunk," he remarked. "And I like the way you think things through. What would you say to our joining forces in Florida? Terry can't object to that, while he's in Mexico."

Nancy agreed willingly, and the professor told her that the study group would have their headquarters at the Southern Skies Guest House in Miami. From there, they would take trips to museums and Indian villages to study the culture of present-day Seminoles.

"Of course I'll do a bit of detective work on the side," he told Nancy, and added slyly, "I suppose you'd like permission to do the same?"

Nancy was thrilled. Everything was turning out so well!

"And now that I've let you in on my secret,

young lady," Dr. Anderson said, "how about telling me yours? What is your special project in Miami?"

"I'm afraid it's not very definite," Nancy admitted ruefully.

She told him about her discovery that the Wangells and Wilfred Porterly were heading for Florida. She also showed him the diary drawing which might possibly have a connection with the treasure.

"Of course it's just a hunch," Nancy said. "But if there is a Black Key down there, I think it may be the hiding place we're seeking. I'd like permission to hunt for it."

The professor stared in horror. "Explore the Keys—by yourself?"

Nancy laughed. "Not exactly. I was hoping you'd give Fran Oakes and me a separate assignment. We could study Indians too—the ancient Indians on the Keys."

Anderson shook his head. "That would still be unwise. Two girls alone!"

"Fran has a cousin, Jack Walker, who lives in Miami," Nancy explained eagerly. "He has a boat, and knows the bay. He could act as guide and protector."

Dr. Anderson smiled. "That's different," he said. "I'll talk to Miss Oakes's cousin when we get to Miami, and if he seems the proper sort, I think we can arrange things."

After that, the professor yawned a few times and dropped off into a doze. Even Nancy, excited as she was, at last went to sleep in her chair. When she awakened, the morning sun was peeking over the Atlantic horizon.

The other students were already awake, excitedly scanning the view far below them. Nancy left her place by the professor and walked back to take the vacant seat beside Fran Oakes.

"Pines and lakes and palm trees," Fran said. "We must be over Florida."

Nancy told her friend that Dr. Anderson might allow them to go exploring together, on a field trip of their own.

"Do you think Jack Walker would take us in his motorboat?" she asked.

"He'd love to!" Fran declared.

She had hardly finished speaking, when the plane lurched suddenly. The next moment Nancy was conscious of a queer sensation in her stomach. Then she realized that the plane had dropped several feet and was going into a nose dive!

After anxious seconds, which seemed hours, the craft righted itself. At the same time, another plane whizzed overhead.

Fran managed a feeble grin. "Looks as if we had a near collision."

"Whatever it was, I didn't care for it," Nancy

declared. "Our pilot must have been dodging that other fellow."

Several students were talking excitedly.

"What happened?"

"Is something wrong?"

"I nearly had heart failure!"

As several arose, the hostess said, "Keep your seats, please." She started up the aisle toward the pilot's cabin.

Marilyn, who was sitting across from Nancy, leaned over and whispered, "I don't want to be a wet blanket, but I've flown lots of times, and I don't like the way this plane is acting. Listen to the motors."

In a few seconds the hostess reappeared. Her face was grim as she addressed the passengers.

"Fasten your safety belts. We may have to make a forced landing."

She had hardly taken her own seat, when the transport started behaving crazily. It lost altitude rapidly, at the same time vibrating as though the engines were conking out.

The plane started to drop!

CHAPTER XX

The Helpful Fisherman

THE plane sideslipped, flattened out, then shot downward again. The earth seemed to be rushing up to meet Nancy and the other passengers. A safe landing now would be a miracle.

Nancy, her heart quaking, looked below. They were heading for an area of small lakes. In the center of one was a small island. It was this bit of land on which the pilot apparently was trying to come down.

Ten seconds later there was a mighty jolt, a bounce, a short run, then a terrific splash. The light was blacked out.

In the silence that followed, everyone expected a flood to rush in, but nothing happened. Then Nancy and the others realized that the plane was not under water.

The pilot had performed the miracle! He had landed on the tiny island, and brought his craft to a stop on the marshy shore. The blackout had been caused by an eruption of mud.

Fran was the first one to speak. "Are you all right, Nancy?" she asked, anxiously searching for the other's hand.

Nancy was unfastening her safety belt. But she squeezed her friend's hand reassuringly. "Yes. And you?"

"I guess I'm all right. Gave my neck an awful twist."

A moment later the pilot and the copilot went past them and opened the door. As each passenger got out in the muddy water, the pilot asked about injuries. No one had received more than a bad fright and a shaking up.

"Thank goodness!" Dr. Anderson breathed a sigh of relief. "That was a wonderful feat of airmanship," he said to the pilot. "What happened?"

The pilot narrowed his eyes. "I'd better not give my opinion until there's been an investigation. I radioed in. It was mighty queer, that other plane buzzing me the way it did. Just as if the pilot wanted to get me into trouble."

Nancy looked at Dr. Anderson. She wondered if the "trouble" had anything to do with them. Had Juarez and his cronies learned that she and the professor were heading for Miami and had taken this desperate method of keeping them away?

Meanwhile, Fran and Marilyn were surveying the spot where they had come down. It was bleak and uninhabited.

"How are we ever going to get off this island?" Fran asked the pilot.

"There are always people in boats cruising around. There's one right now. I think it's heading this way."

In a short time the small cruiser came alongside. A husky, suntanned skipper called out:

"Anybody hurt? I saw you come down."

"We're still alive, thanks to our pilot," said Dr. Anderson. "Only shaken up. How far are we from Miami?"

"Plenty far. I'll take you to Moore Haven. I can do it in two trips. You can get a bus there."

While half the suitcases were being loaded into the cruiser, Nancy overheard the pilot talking to Dr. Anderson in a low undertone. She thought she heard him say something about the controls.

"First passengers aboard!" the skipper called.

The copilot and the hostess went with the first group. Dr. Anderson waited with Nancy and the other students until the cruiser returned. When they reached Moore Haven, the professor telephoned to charter a bus. After a hearty meal, which was both breakfast and lunch, the travelers started for Miami.

The Southern Skies Guest House, where Nancy and five other girls were to stay, proved to be a very attractive place. Its palm-studded yard sloped to the rim of a pleasant inland waterway.

"Jack can bring his motorboat right to our door, Nancy," cried Fran Oakes happily.

Mrs. Young, the owner, was solicitous when she heard what had happened to her guests. She showed Nancy and her friends to three double rooms, then told them to make themselves comfortable. The girls thanked her and started to unpack.

"My lovely new shoes," groaned Marilyn, looking down. "They're ruined from getting out in that mud."

"And it's not only shoes," stated Grace James. "My runless stockings are full of holes."

But little permanent damage had been done. After the girls had spent an hour in Mrs. Young's laundry, the clothes they had worn hung in sweet-smelling closets, fresh and ready to wear again.

At supper that evening the girls met Dr. Anderson, and his students assembled in the dining room of a hotel up the street. The professor had bought a copy of a Miami evening paper, which gave an account of the accident.

"Only the extraordinary skill of the pilot saved the lives of the passengers," it stated.

According to investigators, the plane's wing control cable had snapped. "It is believed this break occurred during the violent maneuver the pilot was forced to make when he nose-dived to avoid another plane."

"Does it tell who was piloting the other plane?" Grace asked.

Dr. Anderson shook his head. "It says, 'The identity of the plane passing overhead has not been established because it carried no identification numbers.' "

Nancy thought again of her enemies. Were they to blame? If the investigators were right, how clever Juarez and his friends were! Instead of tampering with the plane on the ground, they had tried another trick which no one could pin on them.

She was aroused from her thoughts by Fran, who told her that Jack Walker was coming to the hotel at eight o'clock.

Jack proved to be a good-looking person in his early thirties, serious-eyed and athletic. Professor Anderson liked him at once.

"Miss Oakes and Miss Drew want to arrange their own field trip," he said. "If you can give them some time, I'll grant permission."

"I'll take the job—my muscles are strong." Jack grinned. "But one shouldn't come to Florida without having fun, too."

Next morning he insisted that the girls go water skiing before starting on their expedition. They donned bathing suits and joined him in his swift little craft.

He took them to the bay and idled the engine at a dock while the girls put on their skis. Then they started off. Nancy leaned back on her skis and held the lines taut, as the boat gained speed. It was exciting!

Near them were a couple who proved to be experts at the sport. They skied side by side, holding hands. They skimmed along on one foot, while they held the other aloft, and they rode "double" on a single pair of skis.

"Do you think I could ever learn to do that, Jack?" Nancy laughed, when at last they had had enough, and returned to the dock to stretch out and rest.

"It's not easy," he answered.

"I wish we could do that research of yours on water skis," Fran said, sighing.

Jack wanted to know what the research job was. "It had better be interesting," he teased.

"Nancy is treasure hunting," Fran explained. "She's looking for an island called Black Key. Know where it is?"

"Never heard of it. But I know the right man to tell her. His name is Two Line Parker."

"What a funny name!" Fran giggled.

Jack took them to see the bearded old fisherman, who lived in a tiny, white cottage on the water front. His eyes twinkling, he told them how he had received his curious nickname.

"I kin manage two lines at once," he boasted,

"just as easy as most folks handle one. Tell you 'bout the time I got me two big fish, one on the left side of the boat, one on the right side. They were tuggin' so hard, I thought they'd pull me clean apart."

"Did you bring both fish in?" Nancy asked.

"Sure did," said Two Line. "I just tied those two lines together and let the fish fight it out. When they got tired, I pulled 'em in easy."

The old fisherman laughed uproariously and winked at Jack. Then he asked what he could do for them.

"This young lady," said Jack, indicating Nancy, "is looking for treasure on the Florida Keys. Have you any ideas, Two Line?"

The old man became thoughtful. "I don't rightly know where to lay my hands on any at the present. But a heap of treasure has been buried time and agin on the Keys."

"What kind of treasure?" Fran asked.

"Smugglers' stuff. The Keys used to be a great place for smugglers. And then there were the pirates."

"Real pirates?" Fran gasped.

"Real and bold and bad, miss. They'd make raids on the cargo ships that passed thisaway."

"Didn't our Navy try to capture the pirates?"

Two Line Parker chuckled. "Sure, but for a long time they couldn't catch 'em. Those pirates was smart. They used shallow boats so they could sneak into the narrow channels of the Keys. They'd hole up there, after they'd made a raid. The big ships couldn't follow 'em. They'd have grounded if they had."

Jack asked who had finally got rid of the pirates.

"Commodore Parker, back in 1824. He built a fleet of barges and some light-draft schooners. Went after those pirates and cleaned 'em out in no time."

"And that was the last of the pirates?" Fran asked.

Two Line Parker smiled wryly. "I wouldn't say that. Ever hear of the Florida reef wreckers?"

The girls shook their heads.

"I used to know a couple of 'em myself. Wrecking captains, they was called. Hear 'em talk, you'd think they was kind and honest. They'd keep boats ready. When there was a wreck, they'd sail out and rescue the folks on the doomed ship."

"What was wrong with that?" Jack wanted to know.

Two Line Parker snorted. "It wasn't just the folks they wanted to save, Jack. It was the cargo. Why, there was plenty of wreckers in the old days, what would lure ships onto the reefs at night with false signals. Wreck 'em on purpose, for the cargo."

"How horrible!" Nancy cried indignantly.

"So you see, all sorts of things have happened on the Keys. Treasure hid and treasure stolen, I reckon. Any special Key you were thinkin' of, young lady?"

"Do you know of a Black Key?"

Two Line Parker scratched his head. "Never heard tell of that one. There's Ramrod Key and Bonefish Key and Fat Deer Key. There's Tea Table Key, Sugar Loaf and Little Torch Key. I could name you hundreds. But Black Key—"

Then suddenly the old fisherman remembered something. "I tell you what, though. There's that Key where the *Black Falcon* was sunk, back in the eighties, in a hurricane. I never heard a name for it, but Black Key'd be a good name on account of the *Black Falcon*."

Nancy was very much excited now. This must be the place for which she was searching!

"But if I were you, young lady, I'd—" Two Line paused, shaking his head.

"You'd what?" Nancy prompted him.

"I'd stay away from there. I'd stay as far away as I could get."

CHAPTER XXI

The Elusive Island

INSTEAD of being frightened by the fisherman's warning, Nancy found her curiosity even more aroused in the island. She asked Two Line Parker why he had advised her to stay away from it.

"Stories they tell," he answered. "The place is haunted, some folks think."

The old man rubbed his chin.

"Take that ship, the *Black Falcon*, the night she sank. I've heard a couple of Indians talk about it. They say a fire rose up out of her even when she was under water. And after that it rained frogs."

"Frogs?" echoed Jack Walker, and Nancy wondered if the old man's mind were not wandering.

"You don't believe me," Two Line said. "Well, it ain't just me that says so. It's writ down, sure enough, in a book."

"Who wrote it down?" Nancy asked suspiciously.

Old Two Line nodded his head wisely. "Old

sailor down here. Dead now. Lived on the Keys for years, just writin' everything down. Stories the Indians told mostly. He knew their language like his own, and Spanish, too."

The old man's final sentence caught Nancy's attention.

"Who was he? What was his name?" she queried.

"Evans, they called him. Never knew his first name. He went everywheres listenin' to stories and writin' 'em down."

"Had he been a sea captain?" Nancy asked excitedly.

"I don't rightly know. Never talked about himself. Some say just a sailor what had got in trouble. When I knowed him, he'd lived around here for years."

"And he kept a diary?"

"Maybe that's what it was. He made drawin's, too. He'd fool hours away, adrawin' and ascribblin'. But he'd never show that book of his to nobody."

The old man babbled on about Indians and shipwrecks, and about how, way back in 1911, a cache of pirates' gold was found on Grassy Key— "sixty-one gold pieces in a goatskin bag."

But Nancy kept thinking about the strange man Evans and the "book" he kept. It could very well be the diary Mrs. Wangell had in her possession!

"What happened to the diary?" she asked.

Two Line had no idea.

"Would you please show us, on a map, where the *Black Falcon* was sunk?" Nancy requested him.

Jack Walker had a map of Florida in his pocket. He unfolded it and handed the flattened sheet to the fisherman.

Two Line Parker squinted at the whole shore line, and pushed a calloused forefinger over a scattering of small Keys.

"About here. There's a Key near by, I seem to remember, what's called Storm Island."

Nancy marked the spot on the map with her pencil, and decided to ask Dr. Anderson to accompany her there the following day.

But the professor had other plans for Saturday. He told Nancy that he had chartered a bus for a visit to a Seminole Indian reservation. Fran and Nancy, he insisted, were to join the other students on the trip.

Though she was reluctant to spend the time this way, especially since the next day was Sunday and Dr. Anderson had ordered a day of rest, Nancy found the trip a fascinating one. She and Fran were particularly interested in the dresses worn by Seminole women: long-sleeved boleros, and full skirts made of strips of varicolored cotton, reaching from the waist to the ankles.

A Seminole's house, Professor Anderson pointed out, was simply a wooden platform roofed with thatch. The house had no walls and very little furniture.

The visit to the Indian mounds near Lake Okeechobee occupied the rest of the day.

Sunday evening, while Nancy was having supper with her friends at a downtown tearoom, she decided to make a start on her detective work.

She took a notebook from her purse and found the address Wilfred Porterly had given to Sergeant Malloy that exciting day at the River Heights airport.

Fran Oakes groaned. "Watch out, girls. Nancy has a plan. I can see it hatching."

Nancy laughed. "How would you three like to go on a man hunt with me?"

"With bloodhounds?" Grace James grinned.

"No. Just with our own wits."

"Whom are we going to hunt?" Marilyn asked. "Is he tall, dark, and handsome?"

"A man named Wilfred Porterly and his wife Irene," Nancy replied. "Not respectable, I warn you."

"Let's go," said Fran. "It's a better game than just sitting around at Mrs. Young's."

In high spirits, the girls left the tearoom and hailed a bus which carried them north on Biscayne Boulevard. A few minutes later they got off and after a short walk reached a neat, Spanish-style bungalow.

The four girls walked up the steps and Nancy rang the doorbell. They heard footsteps inside, and the door was opened by a woman with a mop in her hand. She looked surprised to see her four callers.

"Good evening. Are you Mrs. Wilfred Porterly?" Nancy asked, eying the mop.

The woman smiled. "Mercy, no. I guess you're looking for the former tenant."

Nancy showed her disappointment. "Did the Porterlys move out recently?"

"Two weeks ago yesterday."

The woman set down her mop. "You'll have to excuse me. I'm busy cleaning. I have to clean day and night, they left the place so dirty. I guess they moved out in a hurry."

She took a slip from her apron pocket. "I found this on a nail in the kitchen. I guess it's their forwarding address."

Nancy read the words: "Porterly, c/o General Delivery, Florida City."

"I suppose you don't know the Porterlys personally?" she asked.

The woman threw up her hands and made a face. Then she looked embarrassed. "I hope you're not friends of theirs?"

"Not exactly," said Nancy. "We came on business."

She and the other girls said good night and walked back toward the boulevard.

"Florida City," said Grace. "That's too far away for tonight."

"Any other criminals we can hunt? In Miami, that is," Fran teased.

"Perhaps," said Nancy, "if I can find his address."

While the other girls waited, Nancy stopped at a drugstore telephone booth and looked for the names Juarez Tino and Conway King in the Miami directory. They were not listed. When she called Information, the operator said that neither person had a telephone.

"The missing persons," Nancy told her friends, "will have to stay missing until tomorrow. Let's go back to Mrs. Young's and get some sleep."

Next day Professor Anderson promised Nancy that he would accompany her and Fran on their trip to find Black Key. But he could not start, he said, until after lunch.

"Would it be all right if Fran and I spend the morning in Florida City?" Nancy asked. "It's only a few miles and we could rent a car."

The professor gave permission, and shortly before ten she and Fran were speeding through the picturesque area south of Miami.

Parking their hired car along the palm-lined main street of Florida City, Nancy and Fran went in search of the post office. But no help was to be gained from that quarter.

"Sorry," said the clerk. "We can't give you any information."

"I might have guessed," Nancy told her friend. "We'll just have to do our detective work the hard way."

Someone, somewhere, Nancy hoped, would have seen or heard of the Porterlys. She asked a policeman, but he shook his head.

She tried a drugstore, a filling station, and a sandwich shop, but none of the personnel had heard of the Porterlys. After that she visited a grocery and a candy-and-stationery store, again to no avail.

"I don't see how you can be so persistent," Fran said. "I'd have given up ages ago."

Nancy chuckled. "That's the fun of being a detective. You look and look and keep on looking. And suddenly, when you least expect it, you find a clue."

They went next to a small souvenir shop selling Florida shells and curios of various kinds. Nancy repeated her usual question.

"I'm trying to locate a man and his wife who, I understand, are staying in Florida City. Their last name is Porterly."

As had happened so many times already, the proprietor shook his head. But a young boy who was sweeping out the shop spoke up politely.

"I think I can help you, miss. I delivered a

package to a Mrs. Porterly just last week. She was staying at the Sunland Tourist Home."

He gave directions for reaching the house. The two girls hurried to their car and drove away quickly.

"Now we're getting somewhere," Nancy said triumphantly.

But her triumph was short-lived. They found the tourist home boarded up and deserted. Nailed over the *Sunland* sign was a neat card saying: Closed Temporarily. Will Reopen December 15th."

"What do we do now? Go back to Miami?" Fran asked gloomily.

"Not yet," Nancy replied. "Let's look around."

She went to the porch and peered into the mailbox. It was empty. Then she and Fran walked toward the back yard.

In the middle of the driveway stood a wire incinerator. Evidently it had been in use recently, for it smelled faintly of smoke. Upon investigation Nancy found that a pile of letters had been burned. Some of the envelopes had not been entirely consumed by the flames.

"It won't hurt to look," Nancy told Fran. "Here—hold my shoulder bag, please."

She turned the incinerator on end and upset the contents in the driveway. Then she singled out the letters which had partially escaped the fire. Seating herself on the back steps, she began to examine them.

Most of the scraps proved valueless. But one envelope excited her interest. It read:

"Mr. W. Port—" The rest of the address was seared.

Excitedly, Nancy looked inside the crumbling folds of paper. Only a scrap of the letter had survived. But its contents startled her.

> Drew girl and
> the trail. Cover yo
> Will meet you at B
> the fifteenth.

Nancy's heart thumped wildly. *Drew girl!* Were the Porterlys and their friends plotting some new evil against her?

"What date is today?" she asked Fran, showing her the letter.

"The thirteenth. This really sounds like bad luck."

"The fifteenth is day after tomorrow!" Nancy cried. "Oh, Fran, if only more of that letter hadn't burned, we'd know where Porterly and someone else, probably Juarez Tino, are going to meet. And why!"

Nancy put the scraps of paper in her purse, and the girls returned home.

"Nancy, it all sounds as if you were in dreadful

danger," Fran worried as they went to lunch.

"I admit I must be very careful. But if a lot of us stick together, no harm can come to me," the young detective assured her.

Fran perked up. By the time two o'clock arrived and she was out on the bay in Jack's boat with Nancy and Dr. Anderson, she felt better.

They were on their way to the spot where so many years ago the *Black Falcon* had sunk. Jack was pointing out various sights to the girls.

"Over there is what's called a sea garden," he was saying. "It's very pretty. Grasses, coral ferns, starfish, and conch shells."

The roar of a speedboat, passing a few yards at their left, almost drowned out his words. Nancy looked up curiously—and her back stiffened.

In that brief moment, as the boat rushed by, she had glimpsed the dark, sinister face of someone she knew. Nancy caught Professor Anderson's arm.

"That man in the boat!" she cried, pointing excitedly. "He's Juarez Tino!"

CHAPTER XXII

The Hidden Hut

As the speedboat passed, Juarez Tino turned to look back, one hand shielding his eyes. Had he recognized Nancy?

"Follow that boat!" Dr. Anderson ordered their pilot.

Jack opened the throttle. The motor roared. The little boat leaped ahead, its prow out of water.

"Glad to speed. But why?" he asked. "Is that man ahead someone you know?"

"We think so," Nancy answered. "Keep him in sight if you can."

An idea suddenly came to her. The note in the incinerator—it had said "Will meet you at B—." Could that be Black Key? Was Juarez heading there?

They raced after his speedboat, following its zigzag course. Then Juarez disappeared behind a palm-fringed islet. When they rounded it, he was not in sight.

"We've lost him!" Nancy groaned.

They cruised in the vicinity for a while, searching for him, but he had vanished.

"Let's not waste any more time," Nancy suggested. "I think Juarez went straight on to Black Key."

Jack headed the motorboat west, but could not find the Key which Two Line had vaguely pointed out on the chart. After an hour he said:

"Let's have a look at that map again." He changed his course. "You'd have to be a wizard to know this place thoroughly. Shore lines changing. New Keys building up."

"How does that happen?" Fran asked.

"Tides, storms, and shifting sands. And the busy mangrove tree. That's the great land builder in these parts."

He pointed to the junglelike growth edging the Key they were passing. "Mangrove roots grow fast and spread faster. They catch drifting plant life and debris. And so the shore line keeps building up."

"Are we nearing the place where the *Black Falcon* sank?" Nancy asked twenty minutes later.

Jack shrugged. "That Key we just passed is Storm Island. And out there near one of those Keys, according to Two Line Parker, lies the *Black Falcon*." He pointed toward a vista of islets.

"But don't ask me which one," Jack added with a grin. "You'll have to figure that out yourself."

He wound in and out among the islands. But since Two Line had told them nothing specific about the surrounding Keys, it seemed hopeless to identify Black Key, even if it existed.

"All the Keys out here look alike," Fran Oakes declared.

They watched for Juarez. They listened for the drone of his speedboat. But all they heard were the cries of cranes, and the lonely wail of limpkins.

"It's lonesome out here," Fran said. "We must be just miles from civilization."

Professor Anderson looked at his watch. "I think we'd better start back."

Nancy felt frustrated, as Jack headed his boat toward Miami. The hunt had certainly been disappointing.

"But," she told herself, "tomorrow is another day. I'll come back. The fifteenth isn't until Wednesday."

Nancy told Dr. Anderson about the charred letter she had found in Florida City that morning.

"According to that, Porterly and his friends are meeting on the fifteenth at some place beginning with a B. It may be Black Key," she declared.

"Sounds reasonable," the professor agreed. "Perhaps we should come back tomorrow and continue our search. We may be able to pick up Juarez's trail."

Nancy was delighted that he had expressed her own desires. "But let's get an early start," she said. "In the morning."

Dr. Anderson frowned. "You forget I have other students. I'm taking my class to a museum in the morning. We'll have to wait until afternoon."

"How about Fran and I going out in the morning with Jack?" Nancy proposed.

The professor shook his head. "Now that I know Juarez is around, the answer is no. Two men in your party is the absolute minimum."

"Oh, bother!" thought Nancy.

But the professor's ruling did not prove as bothersome as she expected. When they reached the dock of the Southern Skies Guest House, a familiar figure came to meet her.

"Terry Scott! How? Why?" Nancy was dumfounded.

The young man grinned. "Like a dutiful daughter, you wired your dad. So when I talked to him on the phone, he told me where I might find you."

Nancy introduced him to Fran and Jack. "And of course you and Dr. Anderson—" she added.

The older man gave Terry a long, cautious stare. Then, grinning ruefully, he held out his hand.

"I guess we may as well be partners," he said.

"I've been using the services of your young detective on my own."

Terry laughed boyishly. "With the three of us working together, we can't lose."

"But what have you been doing, Terry?" Nancy asked, as they walked to the house. "We haven't heard a word from you."

"I'll tell you at supper," he promised. "How about you and Fran and Dr. Anderson having supper at my hotel?"

Half an hour later they gathered in the big dining room. Terry picked up the menu card and smiled.

"Umm. Pompano steak, corn bread, and papaya!" He sighed appreciatively.

"That's enough about food." Nancy smiled, after a waiter had taken their orders. "Now tell the news."

"First of all," Terry began, "a good lead came from the Mexican police. They told me about an old woman—an aunt of Juarez's—who lived a few miles from the site of our excavations. They had a signed statement from her."

She had admitted that Juarez stole the cipher tablet and Dr. Pitt had trailed him. She knew this, because Juarez had stopped at her place for food to take on a journey and had told her the story.

"Did she know where Juarez was going?" Nancy asked eagerly.

"No. She had no idea where either Pitt or Juarez might be found."

Nancy smiled impishly. "Dr. Anderson and I can do better than that. *We* know where Juarez is."

Terry looked at her in amazement. "In Florida?"

Nancy told about the pursuit of Juarez and their fruitless search for him in Jack's motorboat.

"I'd like to go out myself and hunt for him," Terry declared. "Do you suppose, Fran, that your cousin would take us all out tomorrow morning?"

Nancy threw Dr. Anderson a demure look. "I think Jack might be persuaded. But don't ask the professor to join us. He's conducting class tomorrow—in a museum."

Early next morning Jack Walker moored his boat at the guest-house dock. Terry and Nancy were waiting, and Fran hurried to join them at the last minute, pencil and notebook in hand.

"The prof is making me write a report," she said crossly. "Otherwise, I can't go with you."

Jack started the motor and the boat snorted away on its mission.

"What's the subject?" Terry asked. "Maybe we can help you."

Fran consulted her notebook. "The Florida Keys—Their Character and Their History."

Terry smiled. "All right. Let's start with

their character. The Keys are small coral islands stretching some two hundred miles beyond the mainland. At one time they were probably part of the land link between North America and Yucatan."

Fran looked at Terry thankfully. "Gracious, I didn't know that!"

Nancy reminded the girl of Two Line's stories about pirates and wreckers, and Fran wrote busily in her notebook.

At last the travelers reached the group of Keys they had visited the afternoon before and started cruising around. Finally Jack let the motor idle.

"Hopeless," he said.

"It's a maze, all right," Terry agreed. "But let's not give up."

Nancy pointed toward a small craft near one of the islets. "Could that be Juarez in it?" she asked.

Jack headed his boat in that direction, and they soon overtook the other boat. It proved to be a small fishing cruiser, and Juarez was not aboard. Its only occupant was a sunburned fisherman obviously intent on the day's catch.

Nancy addressed him with a smile. "Good morning. We're doing a little exploring. Would you please tell us how to find Black Key?"

"Black Key? Never heard of it, miss."

"Perhaps you know where the *Black Falcon* was sunk, many years ago?" Nancy asked hopefully.

The man in the cruiser grinned. "It's fishing I like, not history," he said. "It's enough if I know the Keys by their shape, so to speak, and how they're arranged. It helps me remember where the catch is good."

"Well, thank you, anyway."

Jack Walker was about to pull away from the other boat, when Nancy remembered something —the slip of paper she had found in the shrubbery at home, with the notation "5 x 7 and one."

"I have one more question, if you don't mind," she called to the fisherman. "You spoke of knowing how the Keys are arranged. Is there any place where they're in groups of five and seven— and then one Key lying alone?"

The man frowned and thought about this. "Five and seven. Well, I'll be switched! That's the way they are, though I never figured it out before."

He pointed with his rod.

"There's five of them over that way, spreading south and eastward. They're in a kind of half-moon. And yonder there are seven more of those Keys, sort of chainlike. They run north."

"And the single island?" Nancy asked.

"I'm not sure about that one," the man answered. "There might be a single one in there somewhere. I don't remember."

Nancy told the fisherman he had been very

helpful, and Jack turned his boat in the direction he had pointed out. Soon they reached the chain of Keys. Sure enough, there were just five of them in a half-moon. The other group contained exactly seven Keys.

"Now let's look for that odd island," Terry said. He was becoming intrigued, too, by the possibility of solving the mystery of the black keys.

Jack cruised slowly around the inside of the half-moon. There, overshadowed by the larger Keys and at an equal distance between the two groups, was a tiny islet.

Nancy was so excited she could hardly speak. "This must be Black Key!" she whispered.

Viewed from the boat, the spot looked like a small jungle of mangroves. But as they approached, its extent proved to be greater than they had supposed. Searching its shadowy rim, they at last found an opening in the dense growth.

Jack coaxed his motorboat into the narrow inlet. Sheltered by the trees, they were completely out of sight of passing boatmen.

"A wonderful hideaway for pirates like Juarez!" Terry commented.

Nancy pointed out a path that wound off among the trees and suggested that Jack stop. "Let's get out here," she said in a low voice, "and do some exploring."

Cautiously the group disembarked and moved

inland. For a short distance the path wound and twisted among the mangroves. Then it suddenly ended at an open, sandy knoll.

Nancy and her companions stood still and gazed around them. Suddenly Nancy pointed through a tangle of bushes across the clearing.

"Look!" she whispered.

Almost concealed by the surrounding trees was a low gray hut. As they dashed across the open space toward it, they heard a plane overhead. It was flying low.

"Hide!" Terry commanded. "We don't want to be seen."

CHAPTER XXIII

A Burned Letter

EVERYONE ducked away beneath the concealing shelter of mangroves, but Nancy was afraid they already had been spotted.

"If Juarez was in that plane, there may be trouble for us," she thought.

The plane circled the island several times, then droned off. Nancy told Terry she believed it was the same type as the one which, according to their pilot, had buzzed them on their way to Miami.

"Looks bad," he said. "We'd better hurry and see what's on the Key before Juarez returns."

Once more he and Nancy crept toward the hut, with Fran and Jack following. Fran was frightened and nervous.

"Is t-this what detective work is like?" she asked. "Why, you take your life in your hands!"

Terry said nothing, but he agreed. He had not forgotten the episode at the Wangells'!

The hut ahead was about the size of a two-room

bungalow and built of heavy weather-worn timbers. Driftwood from wrecked ships, Nancy mused. There was one small window in the front and a low door. No other doors or windows.

Terry knocked. No answer. He put his hand on the latch and pushed. The door opened. The four walked inside.

They stood in a small room, unfurnished except for two canvas deck chairs. In one corner lay a pile of newspapers and magazines, most of them in Spanish, and a carton of canned goods.

"Somebody's been here recently," Fran Oakes whispered. She pointed to the window sill.

A half-eaten candy bar was being consumed by black ants. Beside it stood a bottle of soda, half empty.

Suddenly they heard, from somewhere in the hut, a shuffling sound. Terry motioned toward a heavy door with an old-fashioned, primitive bolt. It led, apparently, to an inner room, and someone was in there!

"You two girls stand back," Terry commanded.

As he started to open the door, a hoarse voice cried out:

"Go away! I won't tell you!"

Nevertheless, Terry swung the door open. Jack followed him inside. Then came Terry's astonished voice:

"*Dr. Pitt!*"

Nancy and Fran dashed forward. Seated on a

cot was a haggard, elderly man, his eyes sunken but with a determined, fiery light in them.

"Thank heavens you found me," he said, deep emotion in his voice. "But I don't know how you did it."

Eagerly Terry introduced the old man to his friends. Joshua Pitt gave them a sad, wry smile.

"Welcome to my prison cell on Black Key!"

He pointed to a small hole in the roof, too small for escape, and the meager furnishings in the room—the cot and two packing boxes which served, apparently, as table and chair. One of them held several cans of food.

Dr. Pitt explained that Juarez and two other men had held him captive, trying to make him tell them the secret of antiquity and where the Frog Treasure was hidden.

"Were the other men named Porterly and Wangell?" Nancy asked excitedly.

"Yes. Porterly was here twice, Wangell only once. But I wouldn't tell them a thing," the elderly professor said proudly, "no matter what they did, and they did torture me."

"How awful!" Fran exclaimed.

Terry asked eagerly, "Dr. Pitt, did you learn the ancient secret we were trying to find out?"

Dr. Pitt's eyes flashed defiantly. "I know. But I won't tell anyone—not even you," he announced. "No one shall ever force the secret from me."

"But why not?" Nancy asked, astonished.

"Because it would mean the destruction of mankind," the archaeologist replied.

The two men helped the elderly professor to one of the deck chairs in the outer room.

"At least tell us," Terry begged, "how you came to be captured."

Joshua Pitt said that the night following the afternoon he and Terry had found the cipher tablet, he had translated the message on the Mystery Stone. He had learned that the secret was one of evil. He refused to say more about it.

Terry asked, "While you were making your translation, did you drop a paper with notes on it?" He described the symbols of the frog, sun, and prostrate man.

"Yes. Those symbols are the clue to the secret." Joshua Pitt frowned. "Because of that I decided to keep the three black keys. But in removing them from their ring, I broke one of them."

Nancy said that she had the half-key with her. Fingering the ribbon at her throat, she explained that Terry had entrusted it to her.

"How did Juarez steal the cipher tablet?" Terry asked.

"After I made the translation," Dr. Pitt said, "I hid the stone tablet under a blanket. Juarez must have been watching me. As I dozed off, I

heard a noise. It was Juarez making his escape.
I knew at once what had happened and I started
after him."

"Why didn't you yell?" Terry asked.

Dr. Pitt admitted that was where he had made
his mistake. Thinking he could handle the situation alone, he had not awakened the others.

"But Juarez turned the tables," he said wryly.
"I followed him to some old woman's house—she
was a relative of Juarez's. He and a Mexican pal
of his ambushed me, packed me into a plane, and
brought me here."

"And the cipher tablet, too?" Terry wanted to
know.

"Yes. It is buried on Black Key," came the
startling announcement.

"Do you know the spot?" Nancy inquired excitedly.

"I have no idea," Dr. Pitt replied, and added,
after Nancy asked when he expected Juarez back,
"Tomorrow."

The fifteenth! But he might come sooner,
Nancy decided. If the man in the plane were a
spy, Juarez would come as soon as he got the
word!

Dr. Pitt's eyes smoldered. "Juarez said tomorrow would be my last chance. He was bringing friends here to make me tell my secret by
torturing it out of me some devilish way."

Fran Oakes shivered, and Terry, frowning,

looked at his watch. He turned to Jack Walker.

"See here, Jack. We can't leave the cipher tablet on the island. How about you and Fran taking the boat and getting the police? Bring them here as soon as you can. In the meantime, Nancy and I will hunt for the tablet."

Jack nodded. He and Fran hurried from the hut.

Joshua Pitt turned to Terry. "Now that I've told my story, how about yours? I'm curious to learn how you knew I was here."

"The credit belongs to Nancy." Terry smiled. "She did a smart bit of detective work."

At Dr. Pitt's insistence, Nancy told the story herself. At the end she asked, "Why did Juarez bring you to Black Key?"

"He knows this area well. Used to come here years ago, looking for pirate gold. I fancy Juarez is a bit of a pirate himself."

"But why Black Key?"

"A friend of his owned an old diary. That must be the one you were translating, Terry. Don't you remember about the *Black Falcon?* There was something in the story about frogs, and Juarez got the idea it might mean the Frog Treasure and it was hidden here. But they won't find it on Black Key because it's buried else- where."

Terry looked puzzled. "Wait a minute," he said slowly. "The Wangell diary made no mention of the *Black Falcon* nor any frogs in connection with it."

"Juarez showed me the pages. He must have torn them out of the diary before you saw it."

"That's the answer!" Terry exclaimed. "When Mrs. Wangell showed me the diary, several pages were missing."

Pitt went on with his story. "Juarez has the two good obsidian keys, and the broken half. Heaven help the world if he ever finds the other half, and becomes master of the secret!"

Nancy longed to know the nature of the secret, but the stern look on the scientist's face warned her not to ask. Instead, she decided to go outside and look around for clues to the buried cipher stone.

As she reached the doorway, Nancy heard a step outside. Before she had time to slam the door, a woman rushed in. Her strong arms encircled Nancy's neck in a strangle hold and forced her back into the hut.

"We saw you and your boy friend from the plane," she sneered.

Terry reached for her arm, but he was too late. Three men sprang at him. While two pinioned his arms to his sides and bound them with rope, the third stood by dumfounded, as if he had seen a ghost.

"Will! Juarez!" he cried. "It's Professor Scott!"

"Yeah," said Porterly in disgust. "You thought you'd fixed him for good, didn't you? Get to work!"

Nancy was bound, then Earl Wangell went to work on Joshua Pitt. Nancy saw him pick up the soda bottle from the window sill.

"Oh, no, you don't!" she said grimly.

Her arms were helpless, but her foot kicked out. Wangell tripped and fell heavily, uttering an oath as he hit the floor.

The woman pushed the girl roughly against the wall. "I'm Mrs. Juarez Tino," she snarled. "Does that mean anything to you?"

Nancy did not answer. The woman laughed and tried to slap the girl's cheek. In dodging, Nancy lost her balance and fell. Her head struck the floor hard.

When she opened her eyes again, she was alone in the room with Mrs. Tino. Her captor leered down at her triumphantly.

"Wake up and start talking," she commanded. "I've just finished going through your bag. So you made drawings from the diary! Think you're clever, don't you?"

"Where's Terry Scott?" Nancy demanded.

"He's our prisoner, too," was the answer. "We haven't decided which one of you we'll torture first."

CHAPTER XXIV

An Evil Bracelet

To HER dismay, Nancy found her ankles bound together. Mrs. Tino started to drag the girl to her feet, then changed her mind.

"I'll search you first," she said in her brassy voice. "I heard you say you have the key we want."

Seeing the ribbon around Nancy's neck, she tore the precious obsidian relic off with a savage wrench.

"Now we have everything!" the woman cried triumphantly. "The fortune is ours!"

"How can it be?" Nancy asked. "You can't translate the message on the Mystery Stone."

"Dr. Pitt will talk, if we torture you enough!" Mrs. Tino predicted.

Nancy's heart sank, but she was determined not to show it. There was one gleam of hope. Only two of her group had been spotted from the plane.

197

These people did not know that Fran and Jack had gone for the police!

Mrs. Tino dragged Nancy to her feet and loosened the strap around her ankles. Then she shoved her out of the hut, and through some dense underbrush to a clearing. There Nancy saw Terry and Joshua Pitt, sitting side by side, bound in the same manner as herself. Wangell and Porterly were guarding the prisoners, while Juarez dug in the earth with a shovel.

"If only the police would hurry!" Nancy thought.

Seeing that Nancy was safe seemed to give Terry courage to bargain with his enemies.

"It won't do you any good to dig up the tablet," he said. "You can't use it, so you may as well let us go."

Juarez gave him a sneering look. "You'll tell us. But no one will ever find out how we made you do it," he said meaningly.

"The police will. They know all about you," Terry warned him. "For instance, they know it was Porterly who knocked me out at the hotel, stole my papers, and then broke into the Drew home."

"And they know, too, that Juarez calls himself Conway King," Nancy added. "That's how we found out you caused our accident on the road to Emerson. You moved that road-block sign!"

"Count me in on that." Wangell smirked.

Nancy wished she could look at her watch. It

seemed like a long time since Jack and Fran had left to go for the police.

She hobbled over so she could glance at Terry's wrist watch. Two o'clock!

"They ought to come any minute," Nancy thought. "We must play for time." Aloud she said, "You tried to break into our home in River Heights one night, Juarez."

"That old woman of yours with her homemade burglar alarms!" Juarez growled. "If it hadn't been for her, I'd have got the key that night."

"But we have it now!" Mrs. Tino cried, showing it to her husband.

Juarez's face broke into a smile. He signaled Wangell to take over the digging. Then he came and stood in front of Nancy.

"Maybe you were smart up in River Heights, Nancy Drew. But now it's different. Even if you hadn't walked into this trap, I had plans for taking care of you."

"I know," Nancy said quietly. "You sent a note to Wilfred Porterly. But he didn't do a thorough job when he burned that letter in Florida City."

Just then Wangell's shovel made a ringing sound, and a moment later he lifted a large stone slab from its hiding place. It was decorated with grotesque carving and mysterious symbols.

Nancy's heart was pounding. Now that these thieves had the tablet, they might leave the island

and take their prisoners along. And the police had not arrived! She must delay these people if she could.

"Well, I guess we're ready for our trip," Juarez said. "First my boat, then the plane—"

"Your plane?" Nancy asked, still trying to delay him. Even seconds counted now! "The plane that caused our crash landing on the way to Florida?"

"A good friend of mine pilots that plane," Juarez answered. "He found out you were coming to Florida. You and that Dr. Anderson! I wish you'd both been killed!"

Nancy shuddered, but she asked calmly if it was the same friend who had mailed the fake letter from Baltimore, using an innocent old man's name.

"Sure." Juarez smiled in satisfaction. "But nobody could ever prove it."

Juarez made a sign to his companions. Wangell and Porterly picked up the stone tablet and preceded the others down a narrow path. The Tinos followed with their three captives.

The path led to the opposite side of the island from the one where Nancy's party had landed. A small cabin cruiser was anchored a short distance out.

"March!" Juarez ordered.

Nancy and her friends had no choice. They were forced to splash through the water and go aboard with the others. The prisoners were crowded into the cabin, and their ankle straps tightened securely. Wangell started the motor.

"You know where to head," Juarez said. "Porterly's place."

As the cruiser pulled away from Black Key, he chose a seat on a bench opposite Nancy. Reaching into his pocket, he drew out an ancient, heavy link bracelet and slipped it around her left arm. Slowly, with an evil leer, he gave the links a twist.

"Stop that!" Terry cried, as Nancy bit her lip.

"Now, Joshua Pitt," Juarez said, as he relaxed the tension, "tell us what you know. Where's the ancient treasure?"

The metal bracelet had bitten deep into Nancy's arm, but she cried out bravely, "Don't tell him, Dr. Pitt! Don't tell—"

Juarez twisted the bracelet again. Nancy could not help groaning.

"Stop!" Dr. Pitt cried. "I'll tell you. Go to Mexico. You'll find the treasure in Mexico."

Hastily, Pitt named a site near the center of a little-known jungle region. Juarez Tino took the bracelet from Nancy's arm and gave it to his wife.

"Here. You may need this later." To Dr. Pitt he said, "You're going with us to Mexico. Tomorrow morning we start looking for the treasure! If your directions are wrong, professor —*you'll be to blame for what happens to Terry Scott and Nancy Drew!*"

By this time the boat had reached another Key. A red-faced, nervous woman, whom Nancy recognized as Mrs. Wangell, met them. She cried out in astonishment upon seeing Terry Scott.

"It can't be! It can't be!" she wailed.

"Shut up!" Mrs. Tino commanded. "We'll take the girl," she offered.

Nancy was half dragged, half carried by her through a grove to a yellow cement bungalow. Terry was brought in by Juarez and Wangell, while Porterly stayed on the boat to guard Dr. Pitt.

An evil smile contorted Juarez's face as he turned to leave. "My little wife, you know what to do with these prisoners."

He and Wangell left, closing the door behind them. A few minutes later Nancy and Terry heard the cruiser churning away from the dock.

They were lined against the wall, while the women surveyed them. Mrs. Tino walked back and forth, swinging the bracelet.

"See here," Terry said. "Let's be reasonable. We can't possibly escape without a boat. Why not give us a little freedom?"

"You talk too much," said Mrs. Tino.

"I don't care about myself," Terry pleaded, "but those ropes are cutting Miss Drew's wrists."

Mrs. Tino's face set grimly. "We'd better separate these two, Lillian." Motioning to Mrs.

Wangell, she said, "Take the girl into the bed-room."

Mrs. Wangell did as she was directed. The door swung shut behind them.

"Maybe I can get her to talk," thought Nancy. "She's not cruel like the others." Smiling dis-armingly, she said, "I know you don't want to do things like this, Mrs. Wangell."

Mrs. Wangell looked at the floor. "No, I don't. But Earl makes me. Oh, I don't know what to do. He and Juarez shouldn't have kept Dr. Pitt a prisoner. It might have killed him."

"It's a serious offense," Nancy said. "By the way, Mrs. Wangell, where did you get that inter-esting old diary?"

The woman was silent a moment as if listening for eavesdroppers from the other room. Then she whispered, "Maybe I shouldn't tell you so much. Juarez stole it from a man named Evans. After he tore out some pages, he gave it to me."

"And asked you to have Terry Scott figure out from it where a certain fortune was?"

Mrs. Wangell admitted this, saying he also wanted to keep Terry busy, so he would not hunt for Joshua Pitt.

Suddenly Nancy heard an airplane. It came closer, flying so low over the bungalow that the walls vibrated. Mrs. Wangell ran to the window.

"There they go!" she exclaimed. "Oh, I hope Dr. Pitt's wrong that something dreadful is going to happen when they find the fortune! Earl is so foolish!"

Nancy pressed her advantage. "Mrs. Wangell, why are you so afraid of your husband?"

The woman hung her head. "I once stole something. But only Earl and Juarez know I did it."

"I see," Nancy said. "Nevertheless, I advise you to turn state's evidence when the police round you all up. You'll get off easier."

"You mean squeal on the others?" The woman looked frightened. She leaned toward Nancy and began whispering rapidly. "Earl didn't mean to be bad after he got caught once."

"About the paintings?"

"Yes. It's just that he got in with Juarez. Juarez knew he had me in his power. He used to play the black keys on the piano to remind me of Pitt being a prisoner. Then Earl took it up. It was awful—"

The door burst open and Mrs. Juarez Tino stood looking contemptuously at Mrs. Wangell.

"Stop blubbering, you fool, and get into the other room. I have some questions to ask Nancy Drew."

Mrs. Wangell gave Nancy a wild, fearful look and hurried from the room. Slowly Mrs. Tino walked up to the girl, the cruel bracelet swinging menacingly in her hands.

CHAPTER XXV

The Three Keys

ALMOST simultaneously, Nancy heard a roar of rage from the next room.

"You brutes!" Terry yelled.

In that instant he broke his bonds. There was a surprised scream from Mrs. Wangell. Mrs. Tino dashed into the living room. Nancy hobbled to the doorway just in time to see Terry lock Mrs. Wangell in a closet.

As Mrs. Tino flew at him in a rage, she tripped over a chair and fell to the floor, stunned. Terry rushed to Nancy's side and untied the rope on her hands. With her hands free, she wrenched at the knots around her ankles. While Terry tied the woman's ankles together, Nancy bound her wrists.

Nancy looked at him gratefully. "Thanks for rescuing me. I'll never forget it," she said. "But we mustn't delay here."

"You're right," Terry agreed.

Quickly Nancy picked up the bracelet so that

it never could be used again to torture anyone, and put it in her pocket.

Terry, meanwhile, had spied a fishing rod. "Bring a white cloth and follow me," he said. "We'll rig up a distress signal."

By the time Nancy had torn a sheet from the bed, Terry was out of the house, and running toward the shore. Nancy hurried after him.

"I see a boat out there," he called. "It looks like a police launch."

He tied the sheet to the top of the fishing pole and waved it furiously. The boat came toward them.

There were six figures on deck. Fran, Jack, and four policemen!

"That white flag did it," one of the officers said, when at last the boat docked. "We couldn't find you."

"Oh, we've been frantic!" Fran cried. "We went to Black Key and there wasn't a sign of you. We've been searching everywhere."

Nancy knew there was not a moment to lose. Hurriedly, she and Terry explained what had happened, and said they must get back to Miami at once.

"We'll take care of those women at the house," the sergeant in charge said. He radioed the story to headquarters, then told one of the men to take the young people to the Key where Jack had left his boat.

All possible speed was made. When they transferred to Jack's craft, Terry urged him to use all the power it had, saying:

"Nancy, Professor Anderson, and I have a date in Mexico. We must reach the treasure spot before Juarez gets there with Joshua Pitt."

Dr. Anderson met them at the dock in Miami, anxiety on his face at their long absence. While Terry telephoned to charter a plane to take them to Mexico, Nancy told the professor what had happened. His eyes were wide with amazement.

"Do you think we can get there in time?" he asked.

"We'd better," Nancy said grimly. "We have several hours. The others won't begin work before morning."

Dr. Anderson dashed to a telephone and got in touch with a retired friend of his. After a few minutes' conversation he returned to the others, saying:

"Miss Oakes, please tell my students that a Dr. White will take over the work while I'm gone. And," he added, "will you get in touch with Dr. Graham long-distance at Jonsonburg and tell him the developments here? Ask him to come to Miami if possible. We'll be in touch with him here."

Fran promised, then fearfully said good-by to Nancy. "Oh, do you have to go? Something dreadful might happen to you!"

Nancy assured her friend she would be in safe hands and not to worry. Then she hurried to the waiting plane with Terry and Dr. Anderson.

About dusk the three alighted at a small airfield in the interior of Mexico. Three uniformed police hurried to meet them, and spoke volubly in Spanish to Terry.

"They'll have a car waiting for us at the crack of dawn," he told the others. "We'll go by a short cut the men know to the spot where Juarez is heading."

Nancy and the professors were escorted to a hacienda by the police. After a late supper they retired immediately in order to be fresh for the task of the following day.

They were awake before daybreak, and by the time the red sun shone over the jungle, the party was on its way.

Nancy, Terry, and Dr. Anderson climbed into a mud-spattered station wagon, while the police took the car ahead. They rode into the jungle until the path dwindled to a one-man trail.

Terry consulted the police, then translated, "The officers say we can ambush Juarez at Diablo Point."

Single file, Nancy and the five men hurried along the trail. The Mexicans set a fast pace, and it was all the others could do to keep up with them.

At last they came to a fork in the trail. The

police told Terry that Juarez and his friends would have to pass here, if they were to reach the site mentioned by Joshua Pitt. It was suggested they all hide in the undergrowth, and nab Juarez and his accomplices as they came by.

For a long time nothing happened. The jungle air was hot and oppressive. Trailing vines tickled Nancy's neck where she lay, and gnats and mosquitoes attacked her ankles.

She began to worry. Perhaps they were too late. What if Juarez and his cronies had already reached the treasure spot! Perhaps, at this very moment, they were torturing Joshua Pitt—

Then she heard the distant tramp of feet, the sound of a voice. Peering through the dense growth, she saw men approaching. Joshua Pitt was in the lead, head bent, feet dragging. He seemed to be in the last stages of exhaustion.

Behind him came Juarez and his pals. Wangell had several tools in his hands. Porterly held a shovel and a large burlap bag.

As they came near, Joshua Pitt said in a cracked, weary voice, "I don't know the exact location. Anyway, the secret will destroy mankind, I tell you!"

Wangell sneered. "Then that power will be ours. And we'll have the treasure, too!"

"Professor, you're lying about not knowing!" Juarez snarled. "Do you want Nancy Drew to be tortured again?"

Terry and Nancy glanced at each other. Any second now Juarez would learn that his chances to torture Nancy or anyone else had come to an end forever.

At that moment the police leaped from the bushes, followed by Terry and Dr. Anderson. There were astonished cries, a fight, but it was over quickly. Juarez and his two accomplices were handcuffed, then the police went through their pockets.

"The black keys!" Terry cried as one of the policemen held them out. "And the half-key, too!"

Joshua Pitt's gratefulness at being rescued was pitiful to behold. Tears gathered in the elderly man's eyes.

"You are truly my friends," he said. "I should have shared the secret with you from the start."

"We understand," Terry said. "Let's forget it, and find the treasure. Where is it, Dr. Pitt?"

The professor said he had been unable to figure out the exact site, because from his translation he had learned the landmark was a tall stone shaft. According to the Indians Juarez had consulted the evening before, this no longer existed, nor any of the other clues on the Mystery Stone.

"It may take years of digging to find the Frog Treasure," he said sadly.

Suddenly Terry snapped his fingers. "Maybe not," he said. "I believe Nancy has solved the mystery for us. She pieced the story together from the photographs I took of some drawings in that old diary which the Wangells had. Let's see—what were they, Nancy?"

Excitedly Nancy told about the footprints leading to a large pool, with a split palm tree along its edge. Terry translated this to the police.

"*Sí, sí!*" one said, and told them to follow him.

Presently the dense growth gave way to a small lake. There were many palm trees growing near it.

"Look for a marker," Dr. Pitt said, new enthusiasm coming to him. "Maybe that stone shaft is only covered up. The top of it might be showing."

Everyone searched eagerly. It was Dr. Pitt who finally located the marker. The top of the narrow stone monument was barely visible among the leaves and undergrowth. Into it was roughly cut the symbol of a frog!

"This must be it!" Dr. Pitt cried excitedly. "Let's dig here!"

Terry took the shovel and quickly set to work unearthing the shaft. One of the policemen stepped forward.

"Let the prisoners dig!" he ordered.

Juarez was given the shovel. When he seemed to be lagging, the officer prodded him with his boot. Wangell and Porterly took their turns. The hole grew deeper and wider.

At last, several feet underground they came upon a tarnished but waterproof chest of solid silver, richly ornamented. It had three separate locks, for each of the obsidian keys.

"I hope they work," Nancy thought fervently, as Terry inserted the first one.

Terry turned it. The lock yielded. The second gave way. Fortunately, the break in the half-key was not in a vital spot and also worked.

Terry swung open the lid. The Mexicans crowded close, their eyes round with wonder.

Inside was indeed a Frog Treasure. There were frogs of various sizes, made of silver. All but a very large one were set with precious jewels: emeralds, sapphires, and turquoise.

Juarez was beside himself with rage. "It would have been our treasure," he screamed, "if it hadn't been for Nancy Drew."

Dr. Pitt eyed him contemptuously. "The treasure belongs to none of us. It is the property of the Mexican government."

"But where is the secret, Dr. Pitt?" Nancy asked. "The fabulous secret of antiquity that you say can destroy mankind?"

"It will be found," the professor replied, "inside this large silver frog."

Taking the finely carved relic in his hands, he showed the others the tiny mark where one foot of the frog had been attached. Joshua Pitt broke

the foot off. A strange, greenish powder trickled
out. He plugged the hole quickly.

"This substance," he said, "has a terrible
power. Unless we destroy it forever, it will destroy us. It will wipe out civilization."

Terry Scott was thoughtfully taking a paper
from his pocket.

"Perhaps so," he said. "But I hope and believe, sir, that you are mistaken."

He showed the paper to the other scientists. It
was the cryptic note containing the symbols of the
frog, sun, and prostrate man.

"As you know," Terry continued, pointing to
the figure of the prostrate man, "this symbolizes
death. But it can also mean disease or human
weakness. It must be considered in relation to the
other symbols. Particularly the symbol of the
sun."

Joshua Pitt's eyes, now, had an excited, happier
gleam. "Go on," he said.

"According to my interpretation," Terry said,
"the frog represents the sacredness of the secret
rather than a motive of evil. The secret is that
this green powder can heal mankind. Perhaps it
can teach him how to use the heat and power of
the sun itself."

"I think you're right," Dr. Anderson agreed.

For a long moment Joshua Pitt studied the
three symbols. At last he nodded.

"You've convinced me. This powder must be analyzed and more of it produced for the service of mankind."

He replaced the silver frog in the chest. Professor Anderson picked up the treasure, and the little procession started back to civilization, where Juarez and his friends would be imprisoned, and where the scientists would announce their find to the world.

Terry took Nancy's arm. "How does it feel," he asked, smiling, "to be such an important person? After all, it was you who went through torture to solve this mystery."

Laughing, Nancy said she was glad that the case had ended so happily. The thought flashed through her mind as to when a new mystery would present itself—a strange puzzle which later came to be called *The Mystery at the Ski Jump*.

"But The Clue of the Black Keys is not quite finished," Dr. Anderson spoke up, a twinkle in his eye. "Not until Nancy Drew has visited my classes at Clifton. I want you to tell my students, Nancy, that the best way to discover treasure in this world is to have an observing eye and a brave heart.

"I wish all my students were live wires like Nancy Drew!"